CHOOSE THE SLAIN

CHOOSE THE SLAIN

THE LONE VALKYRIE™ BOOK 2

CHARLEY CASE   MARTHA CARR   MICHAEL ANDERLE

LMBPN Publishing
PMB 196, 2540 South Maryland Pkwy
Las Vegas, NV 89109

First US edition, April 2020
Version 1.03, May 2021
eBook ISBN: 978-1-64202-840-9
Print ISBN: 978-1-64202-841-6

DEDICATIONS

From Charley

This book is dedicated to my wife and best friend, Kelly.
Without her belief in my abilities, and patience to see the
process through, this book wouldn't exist.

From Martha

To all those who love to read, and like a good puzzle inside
a good story
To Michael Anderle for his generosity
to all his fellow authors
To Louie and Jackie
And in memory of my big sister,
Dr. Diana Deane Carr
who first taught me about magic, Star Trek,
DC Comics and flaming cherries jubilee

From Michael

To Family, Friends and
Those Who Love
To Read.
May We All Enjoy Grace
To Live The Life We Are
Called.

CHAPTER ONE

Mila sat cross-legged on the living room floor watching Finn and Remmy in the dojo as the dwarf instructed the goblin in combat maneuvers. Penny, the small blue faerie dragon, sat on the floor beside Mila and tapped on a laptop as she compiled the latest research she and Mila had gathered for Finn's next treasure hunt.

The tiny goblin hopped from side to side with her powerfully muscled legs while Finn tracked her from a defensive posture that looked overblown considering his opponent's tiny size, and Mila was struck by just how talented the goblin warrior was. It was a proper David and Goliath fight, except Remmy fought with knives and Finn used his bare hands.

Finn reached out, quick as a viper, but Remmy danced backward just out of reach and slashed at his hand with a knife. Finn lifted the targeted hand just enough for the blade to pass under his wrist, then shuffled two steps forward and reached out to slam a palm into her chest.

Remmy spun to the side and sucked in a breath, then

held it and vanished from sight. Finn quickly backed away from where the goblin had been just a second ago, his hands out and fingers splayed. He scanned the area quickly before jumping back just as Remmy let out the breath in a puff and appeared on Finn's opposite side, to drive a knife into the space he had just occupied.

Finn quickly chopped down with the heel of his hand and hit Remmy's extended hand to knock the knife to the blue mats. She dove in to stab with her other knife. Finn spun to the side to let the knife pass through the empty space before smacking the second knife from her grip.

To Mila's surprise, Remmy didn't give up. Instead, she leaped up onto Finn's chest and punched him in the nose once before he could pluck her off and hold her at arm's length by her black spandex shorts.

She hung there, slowly spinning, her shorts tightening with each rotation, but she kept swinging even though her arms didn't even come close to her opponent.

Finn smiled at the fuming goblin. "Okay, I think that one went a little better."

Remmy finally gave up and sagged in his grip, her arms and legs hanging a good four feet from the ground. "Ya mind putting me down, boss? These shorts are starting to cut me in half."

Finn obliged, gently setting her on her feet. "You need to use your invisibility to better advantage."

He gathered up Remmy's practice blades while she adjusted the spandex shorts and matching sports bra back into place. "I outmatch you in everything but speed, and even that is pretty close. If you want to beat a larger opponent, you are going to have to rely on your other strengths."

"But I did use my invisibility." Remmy snapped the elastic band around her ribs and winced.

"You did, but you were so winded from the long fight that it only lasted a few seconds." He handed her the blades. "You have a lot of things that most people would consider disadvantages. Your size, for example, makes people immediately dismiss you as a credible threat. You can ask Penny how well that works out for most of the assholes we go up against."

Penny snickered but didn't look up from the computer.

"You need to think about things like how strong you are compared to your foe, or how small of a target you are, or the fact that if you can go invisible early on, then it's all the more effective because you have the breath to hold it longer."

Remmy nodded, her long white braid of hair bouncing between her heavily tattooed shoulder blades. "I get it, boss. Think first, then fight."

"Sort of," Finn corrected. "Think now, while we practice, so that in a fight you don't have to think at all. Now, look me over and decide what to do to me before we go again."

Remmy cocked her head to the side and narrowed her eyes, glancing up and down Finn's chiseled body. He was dressed in nothing but the pair of the black leggings he only wore when he was on the mats.

"Geez, boss. I know you like 'em small." She hiked a thumb back at Mila. "But you're really not my type."

Mila snorted a laugh, while Finn turned a little red.

3

"You know what I mean, you little shit. I get enough of this crap from Penny. I don't need it from you, too."

"Sorry, boss." Remmy shrugged. "I takes 'em like I sees 'em." She sucked in a deep breath and vanished, catching Finn off-guard.

He shuffled back a few steps, hands up. Mila could hear the slapping of Remmy's bare feet on the mat, but it went so quickly she couldn't get a fix on where the slippery little goblin had gone. She imagined fighting an invisible foe and shivered, just thinking that a knife could slide into her and she wouldn't have any defense.

Finn, on the other hand, seemed to have no problem finding Remmy despite her ability. He quickly spun to his left and rolled forward, kicking out a foot. There was a cry of surprise a second before Remmy materialized to sail through the air. She hit the mats with an "Oof!"

Finn squatted down beside the little green goblin and offered her a hand up. "You need to remember that just because I can't see you doesn't mean I can't hear you."

"You have the ears of the devil, boss. Nobody so far has been able to hit me just from the sounds I make." She took hold of two of his fingers with her whole hand and he pulled her to her feet.

"Just because you haven't fought a higher quality enemy doesn't mean you shouldn't be prepared for one. That's the whole reason I'm teaching you. You're the best goblin fighter in your tribe, but I want you to be one of the best. Period. Let's do it again."

As they reset, Mila glanced at the computer as Penny put the finishing touches on the file for Finn. Every day for the last two weeks, Finn had gone out and returned that evening with a bag full of treasure. Mila was shocked that there was so much lost gold and jewels just sitting around out there for the taking. She understood that there must be, logically, but seeing it all piled up in Penny's room was another thing entirely.

Finn and Penny had had to reinforce the entire building so the sheer weight of all that treasure didn't bring the whole thing tumbling down. As of right now, they estimated that there were just over twelve tons of precious metal and stones piled in the center of Penny's room. Any ordinary structure would have collapsed after the second bag had been transferred to her growing hoard.

The front door opened, and Danica came in, shoulders slumped as she dropped her satchel and kicked off her high heels. She wore a cream-colored suit that accentuated her long legs with long straight lines down from the front pleats. After hanging her suit jacket on a hook by the door, she turned into the kitchen and grabbed a beer from the fridge before shuffling into the living room and flopping down on the couch. She unbuttoned the top two buttons of the white halter-top dress shirt she had on and took a long drink of the beer.

"Long day at the hospital?" Mila leaned back on extended arms to look over her shoulder at her friend.

Danica waved a hand, and her concealment spell fell away to reveal her long, pointed elven ears and her dwarven prosthetic arm. "Yeah, it was a rough one, but it had its moments. I had a kid that wasn't going to make it two months without a miracle. Brain tumor. The mom hadn't realized anything was wrong until the little guy started having seizures."

"Oh, that is rough," Mila said compassionately. "What did you end up doing?"

Danica smiled. "Since I was the first doctor they saw, I gave the little guy a miracle."

She waggled her mechanical fingers and blue magical energies danced between them. "I told her he was dehydrated and that we would give him an IV before sending him home. Sometimes it's good to be a doctor. But I was still on my feet for ten hours."

With a groan, she put her feet up on the coffee table.

Mila chuckled, then circled around to sit on the couch beside Danica. She waved for Danica to put her feet in her lap. "You're going to get caught one of these days."

Danica swung her legs over and leaned back on the arm of the couch with a satisfied moan.

"What are they going to say? That I used magic? We both know Peabrains can't even comprehend the idea. Besides, that's one little boy who gets to grow up and make something of himself. Oh, yeah. That's the stuff. You're too good to me." Her eyes rolled up as Mila started kneading the ball of her foot.

"Well, you at least deserve a foot rub for saving that little guy's life. Speaking of foot rubs. Where's Phil tonight?"

"Working the graveyard shift at the morgue."

"Isn't every shift at the morgue the graveyard shift?" Mila chuckled.

"I would tell you how bad a person you are for telling that joke, but I don't want you to stop rubbing my foot." Danica took another drink of beer as Mila laughed.

Finn and Remmy continued their practice for another

twenty minutes while Mila and Danica caught up on the day, then Remmy bade them all goodnight and skipped out the front door.

Penny finished up the file for Finn while the tall dwarf pulled on a t-shirt and grabbed a beer for himself, then came over to sit on the couch beside Mila.

"How's Remmy doing?" Mila patted his knee affectionately.

"Really well." Finn raised his eyebrows. "I was shocked at how quick she can be when she's focused. She genuinely almost landed a few hits on me. If I can just get her to think ahead and plan her attacks instead of reacting to a fight, I think she could be one of the best fighters I've ever seen."

Danica switched feet in Mila's lap, then groaned as Mila dug into her other foot with her thumbs. "I thought she was already the best fighter in her tribe."

Finn tilted the bottle from his mouth and smacked his lips in satisfaction. "She is. But goblins aren't exactly known for their fighting prowess. They usually just overwhelm their enemies with numbers. A goblin tribe traditionally has one or two fairly good fighters that can finish off the enemy while they are distracted with hordes of lesser fighters. But Remmy has a real talent for battle. Probably because there are no wars they fight here on Earth, so she can focus on learning without the threat of death every day. Out there in the universe, it's a hard life for goblins."

"I thought goblins were servants of dwarves." Mila lofted an eyebrow. "Don't their dwarves look out for them?"

Finn grimaced. "The unfortunate truth is that most dwarves are not kind to their goblins. They usually use them as cannon fodder. Most dwarves don't consider them worth the time to train properly."

"Man, your people sound like a bunch of assholes." Danica chuckled.

"You have no idea." Finn picked up the laptop Penny pushed closer to the couch. "So, where are you guys sending me tomorrow? Let me guess; it's going to be in the bowels of a crumbling ancient city full of snake people that want to eat my face."

Mila snorted. "Hardly. This time you get to go to the beach."

He began to scan through the file. "Assateague Island? Where's that?"

Danica perked up. "I love that place. My family used to vacation there in the summers. They even bought a little beach house there about twenty years ago. Well, technically, the house is on Chincoteague Island, but it's practically the same place. Assateague is covered in wild Spanish ponies."

"Ponies?"

"Yeah." Mila scrolled down to the section of the file about the islands themselves. "A Spanish galleon wrecked off the coast during a storm and sank, dropping all its treasure and killing most of the sailors, but the ship was also transporting hundreds of ponies, which are very good swimmers. They made it to shore and have been an isolated breed on the islands ever since. It's quite the tourist attraction when they have the pony roundup once a year."

Finn scanned the info. "Interesting. So the treasure is what was in the ship?"

Penny shook her head, "Shir shee."

"Who is Charles Wilson?" Finn asked the little dragon.

Mila pulled up another file about the famous lost treasure as she gave him the short version.

"Well, he was a prisoner that died about two hundred years ago. In England."

Penny picked up the tale. "Shir. Chi shee shir."

"Okay, Charles Wilson wrote a letter to his brother saying that he had buried treasure on the island, but that was a long time ago. This island looks like nothing more than a glorified sand bar. Landmarks would be totally different after that long. One good hurricane could change the geography for good."

"Well, that's only half the problem," said Mila sheepishly. "There's a lot of evidence that the treasure isn't real at all. A lot of people think it was made up by a guy back in the fifties so he could drum up interest and sell land on the island."

Finn frowned. "Then why are you sending me to find it? It probably isn't even there."

"True, but while researching the story, we found out that there are tons of treasures on the island. People find gold coins on the beach all the time. There are rumors that Blackbeard buried a bunch of treasure on the island. We figured you would be able to find something."

Finn chuckled. "The old shotgun approach? I like it. This will be a real walk on the beach."

He waggled his eyebrows and smiled as they all rolled their eyes at once.

"What? That was a good one!"

"I can give you a teleport in the morning before I head into work." Danica did her best to ignore the joke.

"Hopefully, he can refrain from being funny on the way." Mila consoled her.

Finn grumbled, "You guys suck."

CHAPTER TWO

Mila turned in a circle as she blinked in confusion. She stood in a nice loft-style apartment that overlooked an unfamiliar city, with the sun just rising over the eastern horizon. She squinted as the light reflected off the skyscrapers that filled the floor-to-ceiling view. Beyond the city, all she could see was desert to the left and ocean to the right.

On recognizing a few of the buildings, Mila stepped closer to the window and, from her new vantage point, could pick out the Burj Khalifa towering over the city.

She didn't remember coming to Dubai, but evidently, she had. She looked at her hands and noticed a shimmering haze around the edges.

"Fucking asshole." Now it all made sense.

She must be in one of Azoth's nightmares. He had tormented her with them for months, usually showing her some grisly murder scene or him taking people as thralls. She had witnessed at least half a dozen horrors since their last meeting, each in a new location. She was getting tired of it all.

As she turned to the main room of the apartment, Mila felt her face tighten in a frown. She didn't see the robed figure in any of the common areas, but there was a stair-case that went to a second level. As she took the stairs quietly, a feeling of dread fell over her. She hated seeing these things, but at the same time, she wasn't even sure if they were real. She never saw anything that she could use to identify the victim. Maybe this time would be different. She just needed to look for clues.

So far, she had reported every dream to Victoria and Missy, but without any real context, they didn't know how to verify the dreams either.

Mila was working on a hunch. That was all. The dreams felt too detailed not to be real places and people. This time she was going to do her best to ignore the Drude and find some sort of clue as to where she was and who the inevitable victim was.

At the top of the stairs, a landing with an office over-looked the living room and the cityscape beyond the windows. She also found a short hall with two doors, both open. To the left was the bathroom, and to the right was a bedroom.

Mila sucked in a breath and steeled herself for what she was about to witness, then walked into the bedroom.

The gray-robed figure of Azoth towered over the side of the bed. His stony hands extended over the face of a sleeping woman, and the void that filled his hood stared at Mila.

"I wondered how long it would take you to find us up

here," Azoth said in his million-creaking-doors voice. "I wanted to be sure you were here for the beginning of the end."

"Fuck you, Azoth." Mila spoke in an emotionless voice as she turned away from the bed to look for clues as to who this poor unsuspecting woman might be.

The room had the same floor-to-ceiling windows as the living room, but these had heavy shades blocking out the morning sun. Despite the darkness, Mila could see just fine, a trait she was happy to have developed now that her powers were awakening once she'd solidified her conviction, the source of a Valkyrie's power.

No one should live in fear of a tyrant.

Mila refused to let this asshole cow her.

"You will be happy to know that I'm saving you for last," Azoth croaked. "I shall hunt down each of your sisters and revel in their screams before taking their power for my own."

Mila barely heard to him. Instead, she scanned for anything that might have a name or address on it. Unfortunately, the woman who was about to be consumed kept a tidy house. In fact, it was practically spartan. Besides the bed, there were two small side tables and a dresser with a large mirror.

The side tables had been cleared off, but on the dresser, she noticed a brush, a bottle of lotion, and a small wooden bowl.

Azoth continued behind her. "I shall enjoy our time when it comes. It has been a while since one of your kind got the better of me. I think I will start with the Dwarf. Really take my time with him while I make you watch."

"Mmmhmm." Mila had heard it all before.

She leaned in and dug through the bowl with one finger.

The dream world Azoth brought her to was interesting in that she could interact with things in the room, but not the people. If she tried to warn the victims by throwing things, the objects would simply reappear where they'd been before she picked them up. She had tried screaming and shouting but quickly realized that the victims couldn't hear her in any way.

In the bowl, she found rings, earrings, and loose change, but at the bottom of the bowl, her finger encountered a thin chain that she fished out. It was one of those ball chains that you see on pens at the post office or bank, or what they use for dog tags in the military.

Mila realized that Azoth had stopped talking, and glancing in the mirror, she could see that his hood was pointed her way as he watched her.

"What? Did you forget what you were saying?" she asked, her eyebrow raised. "If you lost your train of thought, I can probably help you out. God knows I've heard your ranting enough by now. You probably were about to start in on how you're going to flay me alive over and over. Or did you already mention that? I have to admit, I haven't really been listening."

Azoth turned his hood to the side as if he were talking to someone beside him, but as far as Mila could tell they were alone, other than the sleeping woman.

"Your insolence just adds to the pain you will experience in the end." Azoth turned the black void of his hood back to her and raised a hand.

Mila had seen that motion before and knew he was about to banish her from the dream. It seemed she had really hit a nerve if he wanted to get rid of her without killing his victim while she watched.

She yanked the chain from the bowl. A pair of dog tags came with it. She scrambled to grab the tag and see the name. She felt a warm power flush through her as her magic felt her need and increased her reflexes and speed.

She snatched the tag out of the air and quickly read the name. Jennine DeAngelo.

Mila sucked in a breath and awoke to find herself lying on Finn's bare chest.

The large dwarf woke with a start and pressed a protective hand to her back as he raised his head and scanned the room.

"What is it? Someone here?" His sharp brown eyes pierced the darkness.

"It's okay." She rubbed her eyes and pushed herself up from his chest. "It was another nightmare. Azoth is up to his usual threats and shenanigans."

Mila had told Finn about the dreams as soon as they started, but she left out that Azoth always showed her a murder or some other grisly scene. She could take it, and she didn't want Finn to worry. There wasn't anything he could do about the dreams, so why frustrate him? Having him be there when she woke up was all she needed him to do for her to get through this.

"Are you okay?" He relaxed into his pillow and gently rubbed her back.

Mila nodded and brushed her long dark hair behind an ear. "Yeah, I'm okay. He's a fucking asshole, but I'm okay.

And this time, I got a name. That son of a bitch is going down."

"Are you sure it's a real place?" Finn hadn't been so sure that Azoth was taking her to real places since she described being able to interact with the environment, at least in a limited capacity.

"I'm not sure, but having a name gets me all the info I need to find out." Mila scooted to the edge of the bed, her toes just barely brushing the wooden floor, pulled her Valkyrie-issued phone from the nightstand, and hit the power button.

The dark room lit with bright blue light as the screen came on. She blinked a few times as her eyes adjusted. The phone had been magically modified to work anywhere and never needed to be charged, but it only worked to connect between other phones in the "Valkyrie network."

Finn swung his legs out from under the covers and padded into the bathroom while Mila scrolled through the phone's contacts. She was used to talking with Victoria about problems, but now that Missy had awoken, Mila figured she should probably talk with the elder sister. She scrolled back up to Missy's name, hit the send button, and checked the clock on the nightstand. 5:32 a.m. Mila groaned and rubbed the sleep from her eyes.

After half a dozen rings, the phone went to voice mail. Mila hung up, relief washing over her as she scrolled back to Victoria's name and selected it with a tap of her thumb.

She didn't have anything against Missy. She just didn't know her all that well. Victoria was the first Valkyrie Mila had met, and they'd talked at least once a week as Mila had grown more aware of her powers and how to use them.

Since Missy had come back to take her place as the head of the Sisterhood, Mila had felt a distance between her and Missy that didn't exist with Victoria.

The muffled sound of the shower coming on let Mila know that Finn was up for the day. She decided she might as well do the same. She put the phone on speaker as she walked to the bathroom through the walk-in closet.

She smiled at Finn as he stepped into the huge shower behind the glass wall across the back of the luxurious bathroom. He looked her up and down as she walked across the white tiles, then winked as he gave her an over-the-top thumbs up.

Mila laughed at his antics just as Victoria picked up on the other end of the call.

"Mila? What's wrong?" Victoria's voice sounded tense as it came out of the small speaker.

Mila put the phone down on the large white ottoman in the center of the dressing room as she pulled open a drawer and selected a pair of underwear. "Hello, Victoria. Why do you assume something is wrong?"

"Because it is five-thirty in the morning where you are. I assume you don't wake up this early normally. Unless you're one of *those* people."

Mila snorted. "I am definitely not one of *those* people. I had another dream last night starring our least favorite Drude."

Victoria growled on the line. "I'm guessing it was more of the same?"

"Pretty much." Mila snapped the band of her underwear as she selected a pair of gray leggings and ankle socks, along with a black sports bra. "The time thing always throws me off. We were in Dubai, but it was early morning, so I don't know if it happened today or yesterday."

"It's three-thirty in the afternoon in Dubai right now, so it had to have been last night. Do you have any more info?" Victoria didn't sound hopeful.

"Actually, I do. I saw a pair of dog tags with the victim's name on them." Mila said, pulling on the bra and adjusting it into place. "Her name was Jennine DeAngelo. It looked like she was on the fiftieth or sixtieth floor of a high rise in downtown. I didn't get a really good look at her, but it looked like she was white—"

"She was Chinese. Adopted by a family in Italy when she was three months old." Victoria choked up.

Mila froze, her leggings half on. "How do you know that?"

"She was a Lone Valkyrie." Victoria breathed out, calming herself. "She used the Reaper less than a year ago and was still settling into her new life. I just talked to her a day ago."

Mila swallowed. "How did he find her?"

"I don't know, but we need to find out before he does it again."

CHAPTER THREE

Mila pulled a red t-shirt over her head as she walked out of her room. The dojo was dark, but Mila didn't turn on any lights just in case Danica's door was open. She could see just fine with the city lights coming in through the wall of windows that overlooked the LoDo district of Denver.

"What do you need me to do?" Mila held the phone up to her ear after taking it off speaker so she wouldn't wake Danica or Penny, though she figured Penny was already up since the little dragon only slept about three hours a night.

Veronica sighed heavily. "Nothing. I'm texting the others now. We'll take care of it. I doubt Azoth is still there, but we can't be too careful. If he's able to absorb a full-strength Valkyrie, then he must be stronger than we thought. I figured it would take several months for him to gain that kind of power."

"How did he get that strong so fast?" Mila walked into the kitchen and filled the coffee pot with water.

Victoria was silent for a few beats. "Honestly, it should be impossible. That much power should tear him apart."

"He must have weakened her somehow." Mila scooped coffee grounds into the filter. "Maybe he used those shackles he's so fond of, though I don't remember seeing any in the dream."

"Just another reason to get this over with. Did you try to call Missy before you called me?"

Mila poured the water from the pot into the coffee maker and hit the power button. "Yeah, but it went to voice mail, so I called you. Why?"

"I can't get hold of her either. Okay, I need to go." She paused. "Good work, Mila. Once again, you fought Azoth and won."

Mila snorted. "Hardly a win. I found a name on some dog tags."

"You don't think he was hiding all that stuff from you in the previous dreams? You kept looking, and it paid off. Don't sell yourself short."

"I won't. Be careful, Victoria. Call me when you know anything."

"Don't worry about us. I doubt he's still there, but we could get lucky."

Victoria hung up just as Finn came around the corner, pulling on a black t-shirt over his customary jeans and black boots. Once he settled it in place, he began attaching his shoulder harness to his belt. The vertical leather straps looked a bit like suspenders, but a two-foot-long band of leather connected the two straps in the front over his chest, and another crossed at his lower back where he stored

Fragar in its folded form, along with two pouches designed for healing potions.

"Coffee?" Mila pulled a mug from the cupboard.

"Yes, please. Was that Missy on the phone?" Finn sat on one of the stools at the island counter.

Mila set two mugs down beside the gurgling coffee machine and looked at it longingly. "No, Victoria. Missy didn't answer. It turns out that woman from my dream is a Lone Valkyrie, like me."

Finn's brows rose slowly. "Really? How did he find her?"

Mila shrugged. "That's what Victoria is going to work on after she and the others go to the apartment and check it out. I need to do something. This sitting around and waiting is killing me."

"You are doing something," Finn said with a smile. "You're training and providing information. How are the exercises going, by the way? Can you feel a difference?"

Mila crossed her arms and leaned a hip on the counter. "I can. How did you know about that technique anyway? Your power comes from the ground, so you wouldn't need it."

Finn had shown her a mental exercise that would expand her available magic by "making more room in her head" as he put it. The exercise was simple, not unlike a muscle exercise in that she would "flex" her pool of magic over and over until it was depleted. When it refilled, she could feel there was more magic available than when she started. It was slow going, but it did work, and she had been practicing for weeks. She guessed she had more than doubled her reserves in that time. Not to mention, since she had to actually use some magic in the process, she had become extremely good at deploying her shield and had found a few other tricks to use in her next encounter with a bad guy.

Finn chuckled. "I do channel my power from the ground, but I still have a reserve of it inside me. Remember that time Penny had to force-feed me stones so I could absorb their magic? Yeah, that was because I was out. Peabrains and elves are different, but for those of us that have to rely on our stores of magic, the exercises are pretty well known."

Danica came out of her room, already dressed for work in a black suit, her hair pulled up in a long ponytail that hung down to the small of her back.

She yawned and shuffled over to the bench where they kept their everyday shoes and pulled out the black heels she had left there last night. "Morning guys. Didn't expect you to be up already. I figured I would have to go banging on your door to get Finn up." She slid the first shoe on. "You still need a teleport to Chincoteague?"

"Yeah. When will you be ready to go?"

She slipped into the other heel and stood up, her arms stretched over her head. "After I have some coffee and a quick breakfast."

Danica opened the cupboard and pulled out a loaf of thick-cut sourdough and a jar of peanut butter. After popping two slices in the toaster, she began to cut up a banana. "So, what's your plan? Are you just going to wander around the island until you feel something?"

Finn raised an eyebrow, considering, while Danica began to stir the peanut butter with a knife. "I guess so. If there's as much treasure as Penny and Mila seem to think there is, then it shouldn't be too hard to find some."

"Then you should probably take some swimming trunks." She pointed her peanut butter covered knife up and down his figure. "You're going to be burning up out in the sun all day in that. Plus, you'll look like a real creeper walking down the beach like some hipster bodybuilder."

Mila choked on a laugh and spilled a little of the coffee from the pot as she filled three mugs. "Hipster body-builder? Why are you so mean in the mornings?"

"I'm not mean, I'm efficient of word. That's a perfect description of him." Danica put the toast on a plate as soon as it popped up, then smeared peanut butter on the slices while they were still hot.

Finn frowned and rubbed his hand down the chin of his perfectly manicured brown beard. "I still don't understand why you have a thing about hipsters. They sound very dwarven."

"How's that, exactly?" Mila pulled a box of Charleston Chew Minis from the freezer and slid it and one of the steaming mugs across the counter to him.

Finn smiled, opened the box, and shook a few of the candies into his coffee. "Well, from what you've told me, hipsters are obsessed with technology that looks old but works like new, and they tend to dress in an older fashion. Sounds like they adhere to tradition. That's very dwarven. The king's robes have been the same since the first king, a tradition that has lasted for tens of thousands of years."

Mila took a sip of coffee and frowned. "You mean he's been wearing the same style of robe for longer than recorded human history?"

Finn shook his head. "No, it's the same robe. Like, it gets taken off the dead king's body and put on the new king. It's the mantle of rulership. He wouldn't be the king without it."

Danica stopped slicing her banana and made a face like she had just stepped in dog shit. "Eww, that's gross!"

"How can a piece of clothing last that long? Especially if they wear it all the time?" Mila found herself fascinated by the anthropological ramifications of an actual mantle of power.

"Well, it's magical." Finn laughed.

Danica laid out the slices of banana on the gooey toast, then took a big bite and washed it down with hot coffee. "You about ready, Finn? I want to leave in the next couple of minutes. I have a shit ton of paperwork that needs to be filled out before I start my shift."

He nodded, rose from the stool, and took a huge gulp of steaming coffee. "Let me grab my bag, then we can take off." He slammed the rest of the coffee back and slid the mug towards Mila, who snatched it up and placed it in the sink. He gave her a wink while swallowing the coffee, then jogged towards their room.

"I still don't know how he can do that." Mila blew on her own mug to cool it down enough to drink. "I know he's a dwarf and they can handle temperatures better than us, but still..."

Danica laughed and took another sip of her own beverage. "Honestly, there's not a whole lot I *do* understand about him."

Mila chuckled, picked one of the banana slices off the toast still on the plate, and quickly ate it.

"Hey! That's my breakfast. There are still some slices from the banana on the cutting board." Danica slid her plate away from Mila and gave her a narrow-eyed stare.

"Yeah, but those don't have peanut butter residue on them."

"Well, the jar is right there. The knife is still in it." She took a bite and sprayed crumbs when she added, "Hans opf."

Mila smiled and pulled the knife from the jar before smearing the remaining portion of banana with it.

"Ready." Finn came around the corner with the large green backpack he had bought in Mexico and reinforced to carry unbelievable amounts of weight.

Mila came around the counter and held up an arm for a hug while she chewed the remainder of her first bite. Finn bent down and lifted her in a tight embrace, before kissing her.

"Tastes like peanut butter." He chuckled and licked his lips.

Mila just rolled her eyes and kissed him again before he put her back down. "Be careful. And have some fun. It's not every day you get to go to the beach."

"I will. Should be home by dinner. Maybe a little later, if I have to do a bunch of digging. What are you going to get into today?"

Mila shrugged. "I have no idea. Maybe Penny and I can come up with some ideas on how to neutralize Azoth. There has to be something out there to deal with infernal magic."

Finn nodded. "Penny's a good one to talk to about it. She has a lot of experience with other magic systems. And if she doesn't know, I'm betting she can find someone that does."

Danica picked up her second piece of toast along with her satchel and came around the island to stand next to Finn. "Ready?"

He nodded. "Let's go."

"See ya, babe. Tell Penny I said bye," Danica said around her toast.

"I will," Mila waved, "Have a good day, guys."

The tall elf held up a hand, and a large bubble formed around her and Finn, then with a pop it vanished, along with two of Mila's favorite people.

On looking around the condo and noticing that early twilight lay over the city, she decided to finish her coffee on the balcony.

"Hope it's not another boring day," she muttered to herself as she opened the French doors to let in the late spring morning breeze. She sat down and sighed. "How long is Penny going to sleep?"

She guessed it couldn't be all that much longer and pulled out her phone to play the game of the month she had become obsessed with.

This particular game involved baking copious amounts of cupcakes in a poorly designed kitchen so that her character had a stockpile of cakes in order to use them as ammunition to throw at slowly marching teddy bears who wanted to shut her business down for some reason. It was called *Cupcaction!*, and Mila loved it.

CHAPTER FOUR

Mila was in the downward dog position later as she worked through a simple yoga routine in the dojo while she waited for Penny to come out of her room. She had already gone through a full cycle of magic exercises and had exhausted her magical reserves in record time. She had moved on to exercise her body.

In truth, Mila felt supremely bored. She had run out of lives on *Cupcaction!* almost immediately, and she refused to pay real money for more. All the shows she was currently watching were with either Danica or Finn, and she didn't want to watch without them. She had considered going to the Museum, from which she was still on sabbatical, but she had a few months left on her year off and didn't want to give them the idea that she planned to cut the time short. In the end, it was yoga or stare at the wall.

When her phone rang, she nearly pulled a muscle scrambling to the side of the mats to answer.

"Hello?" She sucked in a breath, not realizing how winded she had become from the simple moves.

"Mila," Victoria answered, her voice tense. "Are you okay?"

Mila wiped sweat from her brow with the back of her hand, then blew some loose hair out of her face. "Yeah, just doing some yoga. What happened in Dubai?"

"We were able to catch up with Azoth in the city. He was getting ready to move out, but some locals at the Market pointed us to an empty hotel that was still under construction."

Mila's brows rose in surprise as she tucked her legs under herself in a cross-legged position. "You got him? It's over?"

Victoria chuckled grimly. "Hardly. I could only gather six of the sisters for the attack. I don't know if he knew we were coming or what, but it was a blood bath. Azoth was far more powerful than we anticipated. He must have had fifty thralls and Rougarou with him, not to mention his new disciple. She matched your description from that first nightmare perfectly."

"So, the dreams are real events." Mila frowned. When she didn't know, it was easier to process the things she had seen. Now... She shivered.

"Looks like it. To be honest, I'm not surprised. Azoth doesn't seem to be all that creative. His new disciple, I heard him call her Yaminah, is a hell of a mage. She could sling spells with the best of them, and she was smart. Two of our sisters were killed in the attack. Not permanently killed, just body killed, but still. It's a serious blow to our already small ranks."

"That leaves us with eight Valkyries who aren't Lone Valkyries." Mila bit her lip, trying to think of how they were going to fight Azoth if six weren't a match for him and he was still recovering his powers.

"Nine," Victoria corrected. "Remember, Missy is back."

"Right. Speaking of which, did you ever get a hold of her?"

"She showed up about halfway through the fight. Good thing, too. She had to kill Jenny to keep her from being drained by Azoth. After that, the Drude and his thralls teleported away. I tried to track him, but his infernal magic is too hard to keep a spell on."

"You lost him?" Mila sighed, not wanting to have to track him through the dreams again.

"I lost him, but I did get a general location when I slapped a tracking spell on Yaminah. She's been infused with infernal magic, but there is still a thread of humanity in her. The spell failed eventually, but I at least have their location in the western United States. That's why I was calling. I wanted to be sure he hadn't gone looking for you."

"No, we're all good here. I can ask around if you want. The Market is close by. There's usually someone there who knows something."

Victoria hesitated, obviously weighing the danger to Mila. "Do you think it would be safe? What if he's in the city and waiting for you to show up somewhere public?"

Mila snorted, remembering what he kept telling her in the nightmares. "No, he won't be waiting for me. He's made it a point that he wants to take me last. I think he thinks that the anticipation is killing me or something. I'll be fine; besides, I have friends that can go with me. I won't be alone. I was going to head over there soon anyway to see if there was anyone who might have an idea on how to counteract the infernal magic."

"That's a dangerous game, Mila. Just the mention of infernal magic can drive some people crazy with fear. The Drude are not liked throughout the galaxy."

"I'll be careful who I talk to. We need more than our fists if we're going to take this guy out. He took on six of us at once and still got away. We need an edge."

Victoria sighed as if the weight of the world lay on her shoulders. "Good point. If there's something that can help, even a little, we could really use it. See what you can find, but be careful."

"I will. You do the same." Mila considered something before hanging up. "Victoria, you said he was more powerful than you expected. Could he have gotten that powerful on normal magicals, or do you think this wasn't the first Lone Valkyrie he had taken?"

Victoria sucked in a sharp breath before pulling the phone from her mouth and yelling to someone close by. "Michelle, Gina! Start calling all the Lone Valkyries. We need a headcount." She put the phone back to her ear. "Good call, Mila. I'm going to have the remaining lone sisters start moving from place to place. I don't think it was a coincidence that he found a Lone Valkyrie. He or his disciples must have a way to track them. It's really inconvenient that we can't all gather together."

"What if we gather the Lone Valkyries together? The rest of you can stay away, but at least we would have the numbers to fight if it came down to it."

"Remember that Lone Valkyries will drain *any* Valkyrie's power if they are in close proximity, even other

Lone Valkyries. At least on your own, you still have your powers to defend yourself."

"Unless he comes and takes us in our sleep," Mila growled. "We can get others to protect us. We don't need our magic to be safe if we have guards. I can talk with Preston; I'm sure he would loan us a few G.A.E.L. teams to look after us."

"I keep forgetting that you are still new to all this," Victoria sighed. "The Valkyries would never agree to let others watch over them. A Valkyrie without her magic is like a fish without water. They would rather die than be without it."

"Well, if we don't do something, then they might just have to put that to the test. Personally, I would rather live to fight another day."

"That's why you're special, Mila. You don't think like the rest of us. Hang on." Victoria covered the microphone, and Mila could hear a muffled conversation before Victoria came back. "Three of the Lone Valkyries are not answering. I'm going to send some of the sisters over to their places to check on them. See what you can find out about Azoth's location, but don't get yourself into trouble. We don't have the resources to get you out."

"Don't worry about me. I'll keep my head down," Mila reassured her.

"Why do I have the feeling you have your fingers crossed?" Victoria snorted.

"Because you're getting to know me better."

CHAPTER FIVE

Mila hung up and tossed the phone on the mat beside her before rolling onto her back and putting her hands behind her knees. As she pointed her toes toward the ceiling, she pulled her knees towards her face to stretch out her hamstrings.

Going from exercise to sitting still so quickly had cramped her legs a little, and she wanted to be sure she didn't pull anything when she got back to her routine.

A green face wreathed in white hair leaned into her view, sharp white teeth showing in a huge grin. "Hey, boss lady."

Mila screamed and rolled to the side, then bounced up onto her bare feet, fists up and ready to defend herself.

Remmy jumped nearly a foot in the air and scampered back a few shuffling steps, her own hands up. "I figured we would warm up first, but we can get right to practice if you want."

Mila relaxed on realizing who it was. "Remmy. Fuck

me. You scared the shit out of me. How did you get in here?"

The little goblin tossed her braid over her shoulder and hiked a thumb at the door. "Boss told me to practice my sneaky stuff. I picked the lock."

Mila snorted with relief. "He would tell you to do that. Finn isn't here. You'll have to come back tonight when he gets home if you want to spar with him some more."

Remmy deflated, her smile falling into a frown. "Aw, man. Tonight is so far away. I even put clothes on!" She punctuated her words by snapping the band of her spandex shorts. Then she grabbed the straps of her matching sports bra and shook them angrily. "I hate this thing, but the boss man said it would help. If he thinks it helps so much, why doesn't he wear one?"

Mila laughed, picturing Finn in a sports bra. "It's not for men. It just helps us ladies. It keeps the girls in place."

"If you say so." Remmy put her hands on her hips and looked around the room. "So, whatcha up to?"

Mila sighed, considered going back to her yoga, then dismissed it. "I was about to make some breakfast. You want some?"

Remmy brightened up considerably. "I could eat. What are we having?"

Mila grabbed her phone and slid it into the pocket of her leggings before leading the way into the kitchen. "What sounds good to you?"

"Waffles?"

"Waffles work for me. Plus, the smell should get Penny out here. She loves waffles."

Remmy climbed up onto one of the island's stools.

"Doesn't Penny like everything? That's like her thing, right?"

Mila chuckled, then pulled a mixing bowl and the waffle machine from under the counter. "That's one way to put it."

When the first waffle sat on a plate and the second cooked in the iron, Penny finally made her appearance. The sound of her little door opening, then closing made Mila and Remmy turn as the little blue dragon flew around the corner.

"Penny! We're having waffles!" Remmy exclaimed around a mouthful of golden cake and syrup as she waved her fork in the air.

"Shir," Penny groaned, her eyes still half-closed as she landed on the island counter and pointed at the coffee pot.

Mila had brewed a new pot in anticipation of Penny's need. She filled a mug from the dishwasher with the black brew, then dumped a small handful of Charleston Chews from the freezer into the mug before sliding it to Penny.

"Chi." Penny gave Mila a thumbs up before sipping loudly at the coffee.

"How late were you up?" Mila forked the second waffle onto a new plate for Penny.

Four talons came up as the little dragon continued to slurp the coffee.

"Four?" Mila glanced at the clock on the stove. "You've only been asleep for three hours?"

Mila knew Penny didn't require nearly as much sleep as her or Finn, but three hours was pretty short even for her.

Penny nodded and licked coffee from her lips. She reached over for the syrup and used her whole body to lift the bottle sideways and dump a generous amount of the sweet brown liquid all over the waffle. With an effort, she returned the bottle to its upright position before slurping more coffee.

Mila used a ladle to pour another waffle into the iron, then closed it, sending a puff of sizzling steam from the sides. "I know you're still waking up, but Finn wanted me to ask you if you knew of any way to neutralize infernal magic. I'm starting to look into other ways to combat Azoth, and Finn thought you would be a good resource."

Penny lifted her head form the mug and smiled. "Shir shee. Squee shir chi."

Mila's eyebrows rose in surprise. "Really?"

"What id ee ay?" A chunk of waffle shot from Remmy's mouth. Quick as a cat, she swiped it from the air, stuffed it back into her mouth and grinned.

"She said that's what she was doing up so late. She may have found someone to help. She found a note that mentions a family of witches that made a point of studying the races and finding their weaknesses. Evidently, they have been here since Earth first left port." Mila cocked her head and regarded Penny, who had torn a chunk of her waffle loose and now chewed it slowly. "You think they're still around?"

Penny nodded and swallowed. "Chi chi. Squee."

"Louisiana? Really? Are you sure the relative still keeps notes on the races? We're talking thousands of years."

Penny shook her head in the negative. "Chi?"

Mila shrugged. "I guess it's worth a try. So, when do we leave?"

Penny gave her a pained face. "Shir chi."

"Oh," Mila felt a rush of disappointment. "I guess I can just stay here. I was thinking of heading over to the Market to see if I could find anything out about Azoth's location anyway."

"You could always talk to Christine, boss lady," Remmy interjected. "Her people fought off the Drude on their home planet way back when. I would be guessin' that she knows somethin' about fightin' infernal magic."

Mila's eyes narrowed. "Who's Christine?"

"The naga," Remmy said as if that were an answer.

Penny brightened up and nodded. "Shir shee shee. Chi chi."

"Oh, that's who Finn helped out when he was getting me that Favor? She's the one your tribe is guarding, right?" Mila asked Remmy, who nodded. "I didn't know her name was Christine."

"Yeah, she's super nice and knows lots of stuff," Remmy confirmed.

"Okay, that sounds like a plan. Where does she live?"

"We can get there through the Market. It's not that far."

Penny gave a thumbs up and stuffed another bite of waffle in her mouth.

"When should we head out to see her?"

Remmy checked the clock. "Probably not for another hour or so. She doesn't get up until eight or nine most days." The goblin gave her a toothy grin. "We could do a little sparring while we wait."

Mila opened the waffle iron, pulled her waffle out, and began to butter it. "Let me eat first."

Penny finished and returned to her room while Mila and Remmy cleaned up the kitchen. Once the dishes were in the cleaner and the iron properly stowed in the cupboard, Mila finally relented and led Remmy to the dojo area outside of her and Penny's rooms.

They started with a few easy stretches to limber up. Mila was shocked at how flexible Remmy's compact body was. The goblin looked like an incredibly muscular child. Her abs were as defined as a bodybuilder's, and the veins stood out around her bulging arms and thighs. Mila had expected someone with that much muscle to be at least a little stiff, but Remmy was able to touch her forehead to her knees when she bent over, and Mila suspected she could go further back if her legs weren't in the way.

When she had first met the goblin, Mila had expected Remmy to be square and boxy from Finn's description of her. But all that muscle was still very much in a feminine form. Her hips were wide and rounded and tapered into a well-defined but still slender waist. Even though her shoulders were fairly wide with defined muscle, she still had a hint of an hourglass figure. Goblin legs and arms were short compared to their torsos, but not so much that Remmy looked out of proportion. The only thing that kept her from looking like a well-muscled child was the fact that she had breasts. Not large ones, but large enough that she couldn't be mistaken for anyone younger than a young adult.

The most impressive part about Remmy was not her muscles or her flexibility, but her tattoos.

Goblins on Earth had adopted a hierarchy in the absence of their traditional leaders, the dwarves, by marking their accomplishments on their bodies with intricate tattoos, and Remmy was the most tattooed goblin

Mila had ever met. In the center of Remmy's back, a starburst of intricate design designated her tribe. Radiating out from that starburst were tattoos that told the tale of her exploits, if you knew how to read them. Mila did not, but that didn't take away from the fact that there were hundreds of separate tattoos that made up a vast canopy that covered her body from her calves, up the back of her neck, and out to her elbows.

"Ready?" Remmy bounced from foot to foot.

Mila nodded. "Ready."

Remmy launched herself at Mila, arms and legs extended, and a snarl on her face.

"Fuck!" Mila put up a shield by reflex and Remmy slammed into it. The invisible barrier shimmered with golden light.

As she slid off the shield, Remmy sucked in a breath and vanished.

Mila spun in a circle, keeping her shield up and trying to find the invisible attacker. A small grunt alerted Mila that Remmy had somehow gotten behind her. On reflex, Mila poured some of her power into her body to increase her reflexes and strength. Her limbs glowed slightly with celestial light as she launched herself into a backflip.

Remmy appeared with a grunt, splayed on the ground where Mila had just been standing. She had tried to dive in and tackle Mila but missed and face-planted into the mat.

Mila landed behind the prone goblin, dove onto her back, and locked her arm lightly around Remmy's neck. "Thought I was going to be a chump, didn't you?"

Remmy laughed and tapped out of the fight on Mila's arm. "Worth a try, boss lady. Let's go again."

Mila helped her opponent to her feet with a chuckle before setting up for another go. "Just remember, Finn taught me, too."

Remmy's eyes shone with mirth. "Good! My tribe already can't keep up with me. It's good to fight with people who are better than me. Makes me a strong goblin."

"True, though I don't know that I'm a better fighter than you."

Remmy laughed again, true mirth coming through. "Boss lady isn't even close to as good a fighter as me, but she is more powerful. Should be a good fight."

"Well, I wouldn't say I'm nowhere close—" Mila's eyes went wide when Remmy disappeared, an evil grin on her face.

"Oh, shit!" Next thing she knew, her legs had been kicked out from under her.

She ended up on her back with Remmy squatting on her chest, fist raised to strike.

"See? Remmy's good at fighting," Remmy said with glee. She hopped off Mila and did a cartwheel. "Let's do it again!"

Mila groaned and rolled to her feet. Had she known she was going to get her ass kicked by a gleeful goblin, she would have insisted they just do more yoga.

"Ready?"

Mila sighed and focused. No point in regretting past decisions.

"Ready."

CHAPTER SIX

Mila wiped the thin sheen of sweat from her brow with a gym towel, then chugged water from her Hydro Flask. There a sticker on the water bottle read Anthropologists Like to Watch with a cartoon drawing of a creepy nerd in a tree with a pair of binoculars at his eyes.

"We can call it a tie." Remmy sprawled on the mat to catch her breath as she looked up at the ceiling.

Mila chuckled as she screwed the top of the bottle back on. "Sure. We can call it a draw."

In reality, after the first couple of rounds, Mila had been able to reliably channel celestial magic into her body to enhance her reflexes, strength, and senses. Once she had that advantage, the fights became more one-sided in her favor. Remmy had still managed to get in a few good hits as she continually adapted her attacks to compensate for Mila's growing power throughout the bouts.

Remmy flexed her stomach and kicked her legs, doing a kick-up onto her feet in one quick motion. "Wanna head over to Christine's?"

"I should probably take a shower. We did just spar for an hour." Mila sniffed her armpit, but all she could smell was her deodorant.

"Pish!" Remmy waved the idea away. "We're going to have to walk through the sewers to get there. A little sweat isn't going to make a difference. Trust me, no one will notice. We should get there soon. She's always in a good mood after her first cup of coffee, but after that, her day consists of taking care of the glow worms, and she can get pretty busy. Best to catch her before she starts."

"Do I need to put on street clothes, or will this be fine?" Mila wasn't sure what the etiquette was when meeting a naga, but she thought there might be a need for something more formal than tennis shoes, leggings, and a gray t-shirt.

"To be honest, you might be a little over-dressed. Most of the time, nagas don't wear anything—maybe a shirt if they have company over. Not going to lie, you're probably going to see some naga titties." The toothy smile on Remmy's face made Mila laugh.

"I have to say, Remmy. Getting to know you over the last year has been interesting. I could write a book on goblin humor alone." Mila raised an eyebrow in consideration. "In fact, I might just do that. I've been thinking about writing a book while I'm on sabbatical."

"Oh, I can do interviews for it! Being the subject of a Peabrain book would for sure get me another tattoo. I need to fill out my right arm some more."

"Let me just tell Penny we're leaving."

Mila walked across the dojo to Penny's door in the wall opposite the living room. Her room was right beside Mila and Finn's but had two doors; a regular one and a Penny-sized door halfway up the wall with its own little landing for her to maneuver on. Mila knocked on the full-sized door and waited. After a few seconds, she knocked again and leaned in to listen, but she didn't hear anything.

"Penny? Are you in there?" Mila didn't hear an answer. "Are you okay in there?"

Mila bit her lip. She hadn't noticed Penny leave her room while they had been sparring, but then again, she had been a little distracted. No, if Penny had come out of her room, she would have made some snarky comment on their form or something. Penny was a sucker for snark.

Now Mila worried that something was wrong.

"Penny, I'm coming in." She turned the knob and slowly opened the door.

The room wasn't all that large by human standards, but for a faerie dragon, it was a multi-level apartment all on its own. Deep shelves had been built on all four walls of the room with three feet between each shelf and three shelves high. On each level, there were "rooms" that served many different purposes.

The bottom level had several workbenches with racks of materials and components Penny could tinker with to make who knew what. The second level served as the living area, with stacks of books and five large pillows that had been worked into lounging chairs for her small body. Beside each pillow was a desk lamp that served as a floor lamp for the apartment in miniature. Her bedroom took up the top level with a large nest tucked into a corner. It hung over the shelf by a few feet, but a net that had been attached to the walls and ceiling supported the overhang.

And in the center of it all brooded her growing hoard.

A pile of gold, silver, and gems stood a good two and a half feet deep in the center and spilled out into a dome that nearly touched the edge of the open door. They had done the math, and Mila knew there were several tons of precious metal piled in the room.

Mila snorted when she saw that on top of the hoard, Penny had fashioned a small throne out of Aztec gold bars from Finn's first hunt. That was such a Penny move.

A quick look around told Mila that Penny wasn't there. She started to back out of the room, then noticed Penny's laptop. It sat on the second level in front of one of the pillow chairs. A sticky note with black writing in Penny's small tight script had been stuck to the edge of the screen.

Mila skirted the hoard so she could get close enough to read the note.

Mila, I found the location of the witch family I told you about. Heading there now, and hope to be home by tonight, but I might be gone for a couple of days. I have my phone. Call if you need anything.

Love you, Penny

Mila glanced at the window and saw that it was unlatched but closed. She figured that was how Penny had left, so didn't latch the window as Penny would need to it to come back in. Mila made her way around the hoard again, stepped out of the room, and closed the door behind her.

"She in there?" Remmy worked on her cool-down stretches.

Mila shook her head, then went to a side table where her corset holster had been laid out. "No, she's out on her own adventure."

Mila checked that Gram, her sword, was in its slot along with the Ivar pistol and two healing potions. She wrapped the glorified belt of black leather around her waist and fastened it up the front. She had learned the hard way never to leave the house without her corset and the weapons attached to it. Like Finn's shoulder harness, she wore the corset with everything. It had become second nature to have it wrapped around her. "We can head out when you're done."

"I'm good." Remmy followed Mila out into the living room toward the front door. She pulled her green hoodie from the coat rack. Mila decided that in the early morning chill a hoodie might be a good idea and grabbed her own black zip-up.

They stepped out into the hall, and Remmy pressed the button for the elevator. The door opened right away, and they stepped in. Halfway to the lobby, Mila suddenly patted the pockets of her leggings and hoodie.

"Shit."

Remmy raised an eyebrow. "You lose something?"

"Forgot, actually." Mila considered hitting the button to go back up to the condo. "I left my phone and wallet on the counter."

Remmy tapped the very obviously phone-shaped bulge in the spandex pocket of Mila's leggings. "Isn't that your phone?" Her voice had a tone of "I don't want to alarm you, but you might be insane" to it.

"That's my Valkyrie phone. It only works to call other sisters. If I need to get hold of Finn or Penny, I can't.

"Eh, we're just goin' around the corner to the Market. Probably be back in an hour or so. Pretty sure there's no emergency that's gonna come up in that short a time. You humans are too attached to your devices."

Mila snorted. "I don't think I've ever seen you not on your phone. This morning was the longest stretch I've ever seen you not playing a game of some kind on it."

"We're not talking about goblins and their phone habits." Remmy stuck her sharp nose in the air. "But that is a good point. I didn't forget *my* phone. If there's an emergency, you can just use mine."

Mila nodded, feeling more comfortable knowing there was at least a way she could call out if she needed to. Maybe Remmy was right; she had felt a little dependent on her devices recently.

The door opened, and Remmy stepped out into the small lobby. "Give me a sec. Gotta put on my makeup."

Mila raised an eyebrow. She had never seen the goblin wearing makeup before. The thought of Remmy in makeup intrigued Mila. Goblins weren't ugly by any means, or at least the young ones weren't. There were a few older goblins that looked like they had been hit with the ugly stick, several times. From what Mila could gather, the older a goblin got, the uglier they became, much like every species, but it was even more pronounced in goblins. Their pointed ears became very hairy, along with their nostrils, as the years passed by. It didn't help that their ears, noses, and limb joints continued to grow their entire lives until they resembled the classic goblin from works of myth.

Young goblins, on the other hand, while not human-looking by any means, could be quite attractive. If it weren't for their shark-like teeth and long pointed ears, they could pass for an "exotic" looking child.

Mila decided that Remmy would actually be quite attractive with a smoky shade around her slightly too large yellow eyes. Really make them pop. And maybe just a touch of lip gloss.

Remmy held out a hand, closed her eyes, and began mumbling a spell in Goblin. Like a veil dropping from her head and flowing down her body, a concealment spell formed to hide her goblin features.

Mila rolled her eyes at her own stupidity. She was so used to seeing magicals now that she'd forgotten most of them had to hide their natural features almost all the time. Danica used a concealment spell every day when she left. It didn't change the way she looked, just covered her long ears and prosthetic arm.

Remmy transformed from a green-skinned goblin into a good-looking young woman with a tan. Granted, she was still only three and a half feet tall, but her features were perfectly human. Her hair was still stark white and her nose was still sharp and angular, but not so much that they looked alien.

As she blinked and probed her face with tan fingers, Remmy turned to Mila. "How do I look? Like your little sister?" She fluttered her eyelids and made a kissy face.

Mila saw that Remmy's yellow eyes had turned a dark brown, and her cheekbones had become more pronounced, just like Mila's. "Actually, you kind of do. Did you do that on purpose?"

Remmy smiled, showing rows of perfectly straight white teeth. "Duh, boss lady. It's easier to pass as a kid if I have a big sister beside me. The hoodie hides my boobs, but being a child alone on the streets is its own set of problems."

"Uh, speaking of…" Mila pointed at the bottom of Remmy's hoodie. It came down to mid-thigh on her, completely hiding her shorts and leaving just bare leg and tennis shoes. "Do you want to put some pants on? It looks like you don't have anything on under that green hoodie."

Remmy shrugged and headed for the door. "Nah. Only a perv would think I didn't have pants on."

Mila jogged to catch up. "Did you just call me a perv?"

Remmy flashed her a mischievous smile. "Well, the boss has told me what you two like to do on special occasions."

Mila turned bright red and stopped in her tracks. Her shock instantly turned to fury. "That son of a bitch!"

Remmy's jaw dropped. "Oh, my god. I was totally kiddin'. He would *never* do that. Would he?"

Mila went from furious to confused to chagrined in the blink of an eye. She cleared her throat, felt the heat on her neck from her raging blush. "Right. He totally wouldn't do that. Not that there's anything to tell."

The attempt at covering up her outburst was far too little, far too late.

"Oh, shit," Remmy's grin threatened to split her face in two. "How pervy are we talkin', boss? Like on a scale from one to ten. It's a ten, isn't it?"

Mila screwed her mouth shut and walked past the grinning goblin, her back straight and her steps stiff.

Remmy caught up quickly and looked up into Mila's red face. "Oh. My. God. It's an eleven?"

Mila didn't look at her, just shook her head. "*Not talking about it.*"

"It's an eleven." Remmy nodded knowingly. "Don't worry. Eleven is a good number. Strong number."

They walked half a block in silence before Remmy couldn't help herself. "You could even say that eleven is doubly phallic. A fitting number, really."

"Nope."

"I'm just going to assume it's an eleven 'til you tell me the real number, boss."

Mila's shoulders sagged in defeat. If there was one thing she had learned about goblins, it was that they were beyond tenacious. Remmy would never let this go.

"Six."

Remmy's eyes bugged out. "Six? Holy shit, boss. Good for you."

"Wait," Mila was confused, "a six isn't all that high." She narrowed her eyes. "What the hell do you consider a six— you know what, I don't want to know. Let's just leave it at that. I'm a six."

They crossed the street and made their way down the next block in the cool morning air before Remmy spoke again.

"You must have it in a hidden room. Like behind a bookcase or something."

"Have what hidden?"

"The sex dungeon."

"We don't..." Mila pinched the bridge of her nose and resigned herself to her fate. "Yup. It's behind the bookcase. You figured it out. We have a secret sex dungeon right off the living room."

CHAPTER SEVEN

As they stood in front of the blank wall tucked into the alley behind the bodega three blocks from the condo, Mila pounded a fist against the rust-colored brick. She stood back and waited while Remmy pulled out her phone and started up her game of Cupcaction!

After a few seconds, an eye slit-sized section of the wall slid to the side, seemingly into nothing. A pair of large cat-like eyes filled the viewport.

"Oh, hey, Mila," a deep voice rumbled from behind the wall. "Remmy, good to see you again."

"Hi, Wall Guy." Mila felt stupid calling the creature that manned the Market door Wall Guy, but that was what he said he preferred to go by. As far as Mila knew, no one knew his real name, or even if he was a he. "How are things going?"

The eyes seemed to shrug. "Not bad. Been pretty busy now that summer's just around the corner. People are stocking up after winter, I guess. You know how it is."

"That's good."

"I guess."

There was a pregnant pause, and Mila gave Wall Guy a smile. "Can we come in?"

"Sure. What's the password?"

Mila snorted. "You already know who we are."

"I know who you *look* like."

"But everyone that could use a spell to look like us would already know the password. I don't understand what the whole password thing is for. All magicals know what it is, and anyone that isn't a magical wouldn't even know that the Market is here."

"It's tradition," Wall Guy argued as if that were enough.

Mila chuckled. "Can't argue with that, I suppose."

"So, what's the password?"

Mila fought to avoid rolling her eyes. "Peabrains are forgetful."

"Have a good time at the Market, Mila. Tell Finn I said hello."

"Will do." She gave him a lazy salute as the eye slit closed.

Small bubbles formed at the base of the wall, followed by more bubbles that seeped out of the bricks to form the outline of an arched passageway. Within seconds, the arch was complete and the bricks faded away to reveal a staircase that led down into the underbelly of the city.

Mila started down the steps, followed by Remmy, who still had her nose in her phone, fully engrossed in her game.

The wall reformed behind them as soon as they were inside. The bright light of morning changed to the flickering light of torches. As they progressed down the hundred steps to the Market, the lighting fixtures advanced in technology. After the torches there were gas lights, then bare light bulbs that hardly put out any light. The style and tech kept advancing every few steps until they reached the final light, which was a lantern that looked like it had come from the set of a medieval action-adventure movie, except that the flame was obviously magical in nature. The blue flame danced in the center of the glass and bronze structure with no apparent fuel source.

As they stepped off the last of the hundred steps, they passed through the spell that muffled the sounds from below. Now the loud roar of bartering and sizzling meats from the food court created a wall of sound that felt comforting in its own right.

A vaulted, whitewashed space at least two stories high and several football fields in area, the Market was enormous. Several hundred tents were arranged in roughly formed concentric circles around the center of the space, where the food vendors had circled their carts around an area for several picnic tables.

Several blacksmiths had set up shop in expansive tents that housed giant furnaces and anvils. Other vendors made potions, talismans, or other useful items. Some of the tents sold raw materials for spells, or the spell scrolls themselves. Items, weapons, armor, and goods; if it was magical, you could probably find it in the Market.

Mila plucked at Remmy's sleeve. "You need to lead the way. I don't know where I'm going."

Remmy looked up as if surprised that they had arrived. She switched off her phone and stowed it in the pass-through pocket of her hoodie. "Sorry, I hate talking to Wall Guy. It's this way."

Mila followed Remmy, who wove in and out of the crowded aisles with ease. Luckily, Mila was small enough that she could do the same and keep up with the fast-moving goblin.

"Why don't you like talking to Wall Guy?"

"I'm pretty sure he has a crush on me. It's awkward."

"Isn't he, like, stuck in the wall or something? How would that work?" Mila laughed.

Remmy looked over her shoulder and smiled. "I said it was awkward."

They continued to weave their way through the crowds, but an itch at the back of Mila's skull made her slow and glance to the side.

Between two booths, standing with arms limp at her side and head down was a haggard-looking woman. Her clothes were slightly askew as if she had been twisting around in a bed and had just woken up but hadn't straightened out her shirt and pants. It looked uncomfortable, and Mila wondered how she could stand it.

The woman's hair obviously needed brushing, and there was visible dirt on her cheek that she hadn't bothered to brush off.

As Mila stared at the woman, the itch in the back of her head intensified. She reached up to scratch the spot but froze when the itch turned to a chill.

The woman's head snapped up, and she locked gazes with Mila.

There was a vacant look in her eyes, but otherwise, she looked fairly normal, if a little creepy.

Before she could process the weird interaction, a small hand slipped into hers and pulled her back into the crowd. Mila looked down to see Remmy had come back for her and was now leading her by the hand.

"Come on, boss lady. We need to get to Christine's before she's working with the worms."

They made their way through the Market until Remmy led them to a large round concrete pipe. She pulled Mila after her as she stepped out of the Market and into the sewers proper.

The trek wasn't long, only about twenty minutes, but it was confusing. Several times Mila was sure that Remmy had gotten them lost and was doubling back, but every time the familiar passage led them somewhere else completely. Eventually the concrete turned to brick, then cut stone. Somewhere along the way, the sewers ended and became natural caves.

Mila hadn't thought about it until she spotted a faint blue light spilling out of a crumbled section of tunnel up ahead, but there was no light this far into the sewers, and she could see just fine. In fact, she hadn't even noticed it get dark along the way.

Mila smiled. This was one aspect of her growing abilities she absolutely loved. There was nothing scarier to her than trying to fight in the dark. It seemed that wasn't going to be a problem in the future. She felt a little confused since Victoria had said that night vision was not one of a Valkyrie's abilities and had guessed that Mila was able to see better in general due to the heightened senses that came with her magic growing in power. But Mila was sure they were in complete darkness, and she could see just fine. This wasn't enhanced senses, this was a whole new ability.

Before she could think about it more, Remmy led her through the crumbled section of tunnel into the blue glow.

Mila pulled up short, and her mouth dropped open as she stared up at a million blue stars filling the sky above her.

"That's the face I like to see," a husky woman's voice said. "Lets me know how good a job I'm doing."

Mila's teeth clacked shut as she lowered her gaze from the beautiful view to see a woman in a black and red-checked flannel shirt. She was pretty in a country girl sort of way, with curling blonde hair that hung past her shoulders and a mischievous glint to her piercing blue eyes. She held an extra-large cup of coffee and had a friendly smile on her plump lips.

At first, Mila thought she was just really tall, but after a quick glance down, Mila decided long was a better descriptor.

The naga was completely human from the waist up, but her bottom half was a three-foot thick snake body that Mila guessed to be twenty or thirty feet long. The tightly packed scales covering her snake body gleamed in the blue light that Mila now realized came from the glow worms Remmy had mentioned, not from a sky full of stars at all.

"Hey, Christine." Remmy waved up at the smiling naga. "This is—"

"Dr. Mila Winters," Christine finished. "I would recognize you anywhere. The way Finn goes on and on about you when he visits, I feel like we have known each other for quite a while."

She held out her free hand and Mila shook it.

"I hope he's not telling you too many of my bad traits," Mila joked.

"Hardly. If I were to believe everything he says about you, then I would have to believe you were the goddess Shiri herself in the flesh." She waved a hand towards a corner of the large cavern where a living room of sorts had been set up. "Would you like to sit? I can get you some coffee or a soda if you like."

"Actually, coffee sounds great," Mila laughed. "I haven't had my fourth cup this morning."

"I know the feeling. Go take a seat. I'll be over in a second."

Christine slithered across the cavern to a kitchenette that had been carved into the stone wall. She took a human-sized mug from a set of well-camouflaged stone-faced cupboards and began to fill it with coffee.

Remmy patted Mila's hip to get her attention. "You going to be okay on your own? I'm going to talk to my people and let them know I'm spending the day with you."

"You're spending the whole day with me?"

"Duh!" Remmy rolled her eyes. "Finn is better to spar with, but you're more fun to hang out with."

"Thanks?"

Remmy jogged off. Mila took in the details of the cavern as she walked over to the area Christine indicated.

The millions of glow worms all over the ceiling were such an overwhelming sight that she had completely missed the other features of the cavern. The bare stone floor of the space had been leveled and reflected the glow worms in a highly polished finish that Mila realized was not the product of tools or waxes, but a side effect of a several-hundred-pound naga slithering over it for hundreds or even thousands of years.

At first, Mila didn't see anyone else in the cavern, but when she glanced at Remmy, she understood why. The goblin had skipped to the far end of the cavern and opened a hidden door that spilled the warm glow of artificial light into the cavern. For the few seconds, the door was open, Mila could hear the raucous babbling of dozens of goblins. A cheer went up as Remmy entered the room and shouted, "Morning, bastards!" As the door closed, it cut off all sound.

In the 'living room,' Mila cocked her head as she looked at the familiar L-shaped couch and coffee table.

"Something wrong?" Christine slithered up behind Mila and handed her a steaming mug.

"I have that same couch and table." Mila nodded thanks for the coffee and blew on it a few times before taking a sip.

Christine laughed. "That makes sense. Finn bought it for me to make the place feel homier. Honestly, I think he just wanted a familiar place to sit when he visits. In fact, he sent a lovely group of Selkies over and they modernized the entire cavern. I honestly don't know how I went so long without a kitchen. Your mate is quite the noble, making sure that those under his care are comfortable. More than I can say for rulers I have encountered in the past. Please, take a seat."

Mila sat in her usual spot on the couch out of habit, while Christine coiled her body into a pile that resembled a snake-skin club chair. She even leaned back against one of her coils and rested her large mug on the "chair's" armrest. "So, to what do I owe the pleasure of your visit, Dr. Winters?"

"Well, I don't really know where to start." Mila bit her lip as she thought about how to begin. "Remmy tells me that your people have some experience fighting the Drude in the past, is that correct?"

Christine's eyebrows rose slowly in surprise. "We did, but that was ages ago. Why do you want to know about ancient history?"

"Because there's a Drude here on Earth that needs to be taught a lesson."

Mila had expected a lot of things on meeting Christine for the first time, but white-faced fear was not one of them.

"A Drude walks the Earth?"

Mila nodded.

"Shiri help us all!" Christine breathed the invocation with a look of horror on her face.

CHAPTER EIGHT

"My people were one of the last races to be targeted by the Drude and their armies of thralls," Christine began. She was shaken but had quickly gathered her wits before starting her tale. "My people are not plentiful, but we do wield a larger measure of power than most. Even now, there are only five naga on Earth, spread throughout the continents, and that is up from the original four that boarded the great ship all those millennia ago. We live long and lonely lives, only coming together to mate when the urges drive us from our caverns to seek one another out. After copulating, we return to our homes and brood our eggs, but even then, only one in a hundred will hatch. This keeps our numbers low and places a premium on life.

"On our homeworld, however, our numbers were relatively plentiful, and our power made us formidable in battle. We were left alone out there to find our own way, independent of the greater community of gathering races under the then-new Dwarven Emperor's quickly expanding empire. Even then, the empire knew we were a powerful foe, and while not even close to the empire's vast power, we were strong enough that they left us to our own devices.

"Then the Drude appeared on the still-forming political landscape."

Christine stopped and took a drink of coffee before continuing. She leaned forward on her coils, locking her gaze on Mila to be sure she understood the next part fully.

"The Drude were something no one had ever seen before. Their magic was different from the rest of us, drawing its power from some strange place we couldn't touch or access. With this strange infernal magic came abilities no one had ever considered, like infecting the minds of others until they were driven mad, or the ability to suppress magic in their enemies, making them as weak as babes. But most terrifying of all was their ability to rip the soul from an unwilling host and replace it with infernal magic. That killed the person but preserved the body and the magic flowing through it. The Drude could suddenly take naga captive and turn our own people against us, and build an army of powerful magic wielders to ultimately fight the dwarves with."

Mila nodded. "I've seen that firsthand. It's terrifying."

Christine's eyebrows rose in shock. "You've had dealings with the Drude directly?"

"I was the one who found him. His name is Azoth."

"You are lucky to be alive, even if you are a Valkyrie."

It was Mila's turn to be surprised. "You know I'm a Valkyrie? How?"

"I told you that my kind has a greater measure of power

than most." Her lips broke into a coy smile. "That, and your mate may have let it slip while bragging about you to me. Don't worry, I keep my own counsel. Your secrets are safe with me."

Mila shook her head while trying to hide a smile for Finn and his near-inability to say anything bad about her. "If the Drude were so powerful, how did you defeat them? Was there some tactic or device you found to weaken them?"

Christine shook her head sadly. "We didn't defeat them. There was no magic bullet. My people would have become thralls of the Drude if the rebellion hadn't taken place."

"The rebellion?"

"The Valkyries' rebellion."

Mila put up a hand to pause the conversation. "Wait. Are you telling me the Drude had subjugated the Valkyrie at one time?"

"To be honest, no one is a hundred percent certain of what happened. The story goes that the Drude came first, and the Valkyries were a way for the universe to balance the sudden influx of evil. But, when the first couple of Valkyries arrived, they were quickly overpowered by the vast army of the Drude and enslaved. But because the Valkyries are Celestial magic users, the taint of a Drude can only last for so long, and eventually, they can break free. One particular Valkyrie realized she would soon be free and used her time to study how the Drude were able to separate a soul from a body. She took that knowledge and created a weapon that took what the Drude could do a step farther. The tale goes that the weapon could not only separate a soul, but it would also allow the user to reform that soul and force it back into the original body."

Mila swallowed, keeping her face expressionless. Christine was describing the Reaper, but it was obvious that she wasn't certain that it existed. That was the number-one mandate of the Valkyries: keep the Reaper safe and keep it secret.

Luckily, Christine was far too engrossed in the tale to notice Mila's strange behavior.

"With that kind of power, the Valkyries would be like gods, able to choose who had power and who didn't. No one was safe from them. Even the Dwarven Emperor was vulnerable if a Valkyrie could get close enough, but the ones who were truly afraid were the Drude.

"There is a legend that when the first Valkyrie made her escape, she used the weapon on her master and his household, ripping all magic from them and leaving him and his people on a barren planet, devoid of all magic to fend for themselves."

Christine waved a hand. "But that's just legend. The true story is that for whatever reason, be it rebellion or the Valkyries showing up at just the right time, a war started between the two powerful races that still rages out there in the vastness of space. It seems the war still rages here on Earth as well. Once the Drude left our homeworld, we joined the Dwarven Empire and were protected from further attack, though it was at a steep price; but that's another story."

Mila frowned, looking down into her still-full cup of coffee. "What do the Drude's spaceships look like?" Mila suddenly asked. She thought about how they used the pent-up magical potential in Finn's old ship to create a gigantic explosion. If the only way to fight a Drude was with raw power, it might help. "I know the Drude chased my sisters to Earth after it had left on its voyage, so the ship must still be here somewhere."

Christine shook her head. "There is no ship. Drude are one of the few races in the known universe that do not require a ship to travel through it. They can transport themselves and their thralls with little effort."

"How many thralls can they take with them?" Mila asked out of curiosity.

"They brought vast armies with them when they attacked my planet. The stories say thralls covered the landscape like locusts, swarming in the millions, and overrunning our cities with sheer numbers."

Mila snorted. "So the answer is a lot."

Christine nodded. "A metric shit-ton."

There was nothing else Mila needed to know. Evidently the only way to fight a Drude was with more power; something that was becoming rarer as Azoth slowly picked Valkyries off one by one.

They chatted about the mundane after that, mostly about Finn and what he had been up to lately. Christine was excited that Penny was finally attempting to lay her eggs, and asked that Mila tell the little dragon to come visit soon. They spoke for nearly a half an hour before Remmy came out of the goblin den at the back of the cavern and told Mila she was ready to go whenever.

They made their goodbyes, and Mila promised to come back soon with Finn and Penny for a nice dinner with Christine.

The naga gave Mila a hug and a pat on the cheek as they left the cavern. Mila decided she liked the half-snake woman and made a note to get down to see her again soon.

The way back to the Market, while still confusing to Mila, made a little more sense now that she had done it once before. Remmy led the way, and when they were close enough that the sounds of commerce were more than a whisper on the wind, Remmy said she was ready for a snack at the food court.

Mila agreed that some food sounded good, but that she had left her wallet at home. Remmy pulled out a small wad of cash.

"I've got it, boss."

Remmy led the way to her favorite noodle bar on the edge of the food court at the heart of the Market.

It was a rather ratty-looking white-and-red-striped tent with a wooden counter that blocked the view to the prep area were various columns of steam rose and filled the air with a savory pork-like smell. Mila looked up at the sign, which was a picture of a bowl full of noodles and three slices of meat.

"What is this place? It looks sketchy as hell."

Remmy just grabbed her hand and pulled her to the counter. "It doesn't have a name. Everyone just calls it That Noodle Soup Place at the Food Court. You like pork, right?"

Mila gave her a narrow gaze. "Is it Earth pork, or am I going to find out later that it's a slug or something?"

Remmy rolled her eyes and turned to the old man behind the counter. Mila jumped at the sight of him, not having realized that the man was a Peabrain. He was so old, stooped, and wrinkly that Mila couldn't tell what nationality he was. Not to mention the too-large food-stained white apron covered everything but his wrinkled and liver-spotted arms and hands. On a second glance, Mila was pretty sure the apron was all he was wearing, at least on top; she just prayed that he had pants on, without looking to check.

"Two number threes, please. And can you put extra eggs in both?"

The ancient man nodded slowly before shuffling behind the tall counter. Mila wasn't tall enough to see what was happening back there, but by the sound of it, ten people were suddenly very busy. At one point, chopped green onion started shooting up into the air, followed by a ball of cooked noodles trailing steaming water droplets. Then, just as fast as it started, it stopped, and the stooped man shuffled out from behind the counter, two steaming bowls of soup in his hands. He set them down on the counter and slowly slid two pairs of chopsticks and two wide, flat spoons forward far enough that Remmy could reach them.

Remmy peeled off thirty bucks from the roll and handed it to the old man. "Keep the change, Grandpa."

The old man nodded, took the money, stuffed it in his apron pocket, then sat on a small wooden stool and immediately fell asleep.

Mila leaned over the short section of counter where Remmy had ordered to see how many people the old guy had working back there, but there was no one but the old man.

"What the fuck?"

"Come on, it's best to eat while it's hot."

Remmy picked up her bowl and utensils and carefully walked to the closest picnic table, doing her best not to spill any of the soup.

Mila picked her order up and followed, taking a close look at the contents of the bowl. The broth was an opaque milky tan color, with a pile of noodles in the middle. On top of the noodles were two breaded and fried cutlets of meat that did in fact look like pork, cut into half-inch strips. Two brown-colored hard-boiled eggs were on one side, with a pile of green onion and thin-sliced mushrooms on the other.

Taking a deep whiff of the soup, Mila smiled and put a skip in her step as she joined Remmy at the table. "This is tonkatsu ramen! Why didn't you say that form the beginning?"

Remmy shrugged. "Never heard of it."

"What? It's a staple Japanese food. We passed a place that has this stuff on the way to the Market from the condo."

Remmy laughed. "There's nothin like this, boss. I'll eat my spandex if you don't think it's the greatest thing you've ever eaten."

Mila scoffed. "I've had ramen in Kyoto and Tokyo. I doubt this will beat that, so I'll take that bet." She ladled out a spoonful of the broth and blew on it a few times before slurping it up as Remmy watched her with a smug smile on her face.

Mila rolled the broth around her mouth, giving it a chance. The longer it was on her tongue, the better it tasted. It quickly outpaced anything she had eaten recently and blew the local ramen place out of the water. It blew the doors off the food from her Japan trip with ease.

The silky-smooth, savory, umami blast of flavor made her tear up with joy. "Oh. My. God. He has to be using magic to make this so good. There is no way you could do this without some kind of help."

"So, my spandex is safe?" Remmy gloated.

Mila just nodded.

"I know he doesn't use magic, by the way. He can't. He's not awoken." Remmy slurped up a chopstick full of noodles, flinging broth off the whipping ends.

"I thought you had to be a magical to get into the Market?" The pork cutlet was to die for, and she let out a loud moan of pleasure.

"They make an exception for Grandpa. As far as I know, he's the only one. The food's too good, ya know?"

Mila nodded, her mouth full of the best thing she had ever eaten.

They fell silent, the only sounds for the next ten minutes slurping and moans of pleasure.

Mila leaned back, putting a hand on her slightly distended belly. "Fuck me. That was amazing. Why the hell didn't Finn bring me here instead of over to the place that sells fried larvae? Grandpa just got himself a new regular."

"Amen, sister," Remmy groaned, rubbing her belly.

They sat in food euphoria for a few minutes, letting the ramen experience flood through them both.

A scream cut through the general noise of the Market, making both of them sit up and take note. Mila raised an eyebrow at Remmy, who shrugged. There was a second scream, followed quickly by a third and a fourth. Then all hell broke loose.

It sounded like it was coming from the main entrance, but Mila was too short to see over the tents. She quickly scrambled onto the table and stood on her tiptoes, trying to get a view.

The arch to the main entrance's stairway was the center of the disturbance. People were scrambling away from the opening in all directions as Rougarou poured into the crowd. They were attacking indiscriminately, slashing anyone in range, and sending out sprays of blood as their long black talons found soft flesh.

Mila watched in stunned horror as a wave of thralls followed the Rougarou. They were mostly Peabrains, but there were a few magicals mixed in. They all moved in jerks and starts, as if the zombie apocalypse were pouring down the stairs. As soon as the thralls got close to a victim, however, their movements became more fluid as they pounced and began slamming fists into their targets.

Finally, a lone figure walked down the steps. It was Yaminah, Azoth's disciple. Mila recognized her form the very first dream Azoth had sent her.

Standing at nearly six feet, Yaminah had a commanding presence, with wide shoulders and a permanently furrowed brow. She wore her black hair in one thick braid that hung down to her calves and was cinched with a golden ring at the end. Her long black robe was open in the front, revealing simple black pants and a form-fitting t-shirt.

Mila's breath caught in her throat when Yaminah looked up and locked eyes with her. A beat passed as recognition cemented itself in the woman, and she slowly raised an arm to point at Mila.

"Take her down!"

The Rougarou and thralls stopped attacking those closest to them and turned to face Mila.

"Oh, fuck. Remmy, we have incoming. A *lot* of incoming."

Remmy dashed to the closest food cart and snatched a pair of knives, to the protests of the cart's owner. She dashed into the maze of picnic tables and held the blades at the ready.

"Let's see who can kill more of them," Remmy suggested. She let out a battle cry that honestly impressed Mila.

Tents and small wooden structures began to be launched into the air as the Rougarou took the most direct route to their prey, which was through several rows of stalls.

Mila pulled out Gram and activated the sword with a whispered word, letting the golden blade unfold to its full length. Another word of power and her mythril armor rose out of her skin like condensation on a cold glass. She debated using the Ivar but decided there were far too many bystanders for the gun.

Mila set her jaw. It was time to put all that practice to work.

CHAPTER NINE

"How many?" Remmy shouted up at Mila, who was still on the table.

"Three dozen, at least. Half Rougarou and half thralls. Plus, there's a powerful caster leading them. So, probably more than we can handle." Mila looked over to Remmy, but she was gone.

Mila quickly looked around and caught a flash of green hoodie disappear around a tent in the opposite direction from the incoming enemy. Finn had said that goblins were powerful in groups, but fairly cowardly alone. Mila had never thought that would have applied to Remmy.

As she gritted her teeth, Mila let the disappointment of being abandoned wash away. She would just have to deal with the enemy on her own. But when she saw several of the Market-goers open up on the charging beasts, she realized that she wouldn't be fighting alone.

Bubbles that transformed into flying spears or small fireballs slammed into the backs of some of the thralls, to send them tumbling to the ground where they lay still.

Soon, more of the bystanders joined in to blast away at the attackers. Mila didn't have time to see just how effective the help was as the rushing Rougarou tore through the last line of booths and trampled them into the ground.

The fireballs gave Mila an idea. Since most of the Rougarou charged through the freshly made gap in the tents instead of making new holes, she decided now was a perfect time to use some of her new powers.

As she released her magic, Mila felt a heady rush of power flow from the back of her skull out to her extremities. She concentrated, willing some of the power to pool in her left hand. Once she felt she had enough magic roiling just below her skin, she snapped her gaze up and focused on her target.

Mila dropped off the end of the table, let out a war cry of pure determination, and slammed the palm of her hand against the concrete floor. The magic she had pulled together rushed out of her, leaving a void quickly filled by her reserves.

In her mind, Mila imagined a line of intense flames ripping across the stone and enveloping the area between the booth. The celestial magic obeyed her wishes, and a white-hot flame raced across the floor directly into the massed Rougarou.

The sound of howling pain filled the Market as the three wolfmen in the lead were incinerated where they stood. Unfortunately, the rest of the packed beast-men dove to either side, avoiding the worst of the magical flames.

Mila knew she would be surrounded out in the open, and quickly backed into the maze of picnic tables. She jumped onto a tabletop so she wouldn't be at such a height disadvantage against the eight-foot-tall Rougarou still rushing over the burned and twitching bodies of their comrades.

In seconds, the lead Rougarou closed the distance as it jumped over the tables like they weren't even there. Before she knew it, the beast swiped its talons at Mila's heart.

Her shield formed purely by instinct. She tucked in behind it as celestial power infused her body to reinforce her physical abilities so the Rougarou's hit didn't shove her off the tabletop.

Golden sparks showered from the invisible shield and bounced the Rougarou's arm back as if it had hit a trampoline to leave its right side open.

Mila dropped the shield and stabbed hard with Gram. A howl of pain and a slight resistance told Mila that she had hit the mark. With her enhanced muscles, Mila slashed sideways and sliced the Rougarou practically in half at chest level.

Blood splattered on her face as she pulled the blade free. There was no time to rejoice in her victory, however, as three more wolfmen took the first one's place.

Mila charged.

As she leaped off the end of the table, she used the still falling form of her first victim as a springboard and dove over the incoming Rougarou to catch them off-guard.

Gram flashed out to slice the head and shoulder from one of the wolfmen. The other two lashed out with their talons, but she had already passed them and now rolled on the ground toward the larger bulk of the pack. She caught glimpses of bared teeth as she rolled and timed her next move perfectly.

She used the momentum of her roll to spin up into a kneeling position, yanked the Ivar from its holster, and aimed it at the center mass of the group of Rougarou coming through the gap. She pulled the trigger to send a bolt of pure celestial magic into the crowd of furry bodies.

Without sticking around to see what happened, Mila spun back to the two Rougarou she had just leapt over and charged towards them again as she re-holstered the Ivar. The sound of the celestial bolt exploding behind her, followed by the yelping cries of several of the enemy, told her the shot had been effective.

In anticipation that she would, once again, jump over them, both wolfmen raised their arms and tilted their heads back slightly. So they were quite confused when instead she dropped to her knees and slid between the left one's legs.

Gram made short work of the muscle and bone of the Rougarou's left thigh and chopped the limb off just above the knee.

Despite her enhanced reflexes and speed, the beast-men were still unimaginably quick as Mila learned when she felt the sting of talons ripping into her back.

The pain was manageable, especially since her mythril armor stopped the razor-sharp claws from breaking the skin. The mass of the Rougarou behind the forceful hit slammed Mila to the stone floor. She felt one of her ribs crack as the blow drove the wind from her.

Excruciating pain radiated from her back near her spine,

where the rib had snapped. Mila groaned but knew she had no time to deal with the pain. She released a small trickle of magic and the pain vanished. She needed to be careful as the magic hadn't healed her, just cut off her ability to feel the physical effects of her injuries. Pain was an early warning system the body used to keep you from injuring yourself beyond repair, and she had just cut the wires.

Mila copied the move she had seen Remmy do earlier after their sparring and placed her free hand on the ground beside her head, then did a one-handed kip up. As she landed on her feet, she spun to face the last Rougarou and nearly screamed when she saw it was right in her face, the black talons of both hands coming in from both sides to shred her.

Her shield went up just in time. Sparks danced along both sides of the half-sphere shield, and she dropped to one knee.

Saliva dripped from the open maw of the crazed wolf-man, his teeth bared as a snarl rumbled out of his throat. The thick, foamy spittle plopped onto her shield and slowly slid down the magical barrier.

"I can actually smell your breath through my shield," Mila said in disgust.

That just seemed to enrage the beast and send him into a flurry of blows, his claws striking the shield over and over to no avail. Mila took the relative safety of the moment to assess the situation.

Tents and booths popped out of existence as the store owners teleported themselves and their goods to safety. Nearly two-thirds of the remaining stalls were empty, and the density of bystanders had thinned considerably. Luckily, not everyone was running.

At least ten men and women of different magical races still unleashed hell on the horde that had attacked their place of safety from nowhere. They focused their efforts mostly on the Rougarou since they appeared to be the more threatening enemy. Only three Rougarou, besides the one Mila kept occupied, remained. However, they dodged attacks from multiple opponents while closing on their attackers.

Mila immediately saw that the problem was not going to be the closing Rougarou, but the zombie-like thralls that had circled around behind one line of Market defenders. They were about to be swarmed.

"Behind you!" Mila screamed, but there was far too much noise echoing off the stone and brick walls for her to be heard.

The first thrall got to its target in a stumbling, reaching grab that took the elf woman by surprise. She screamed, sending an elbow into the slack-jawed thrall, breaking the bone, but the man that the thrall used to be didn't feel the pain and held on tight. A second thrall latched onto her, and between the two of them, they got a hold of an arm each and began to pull in opposite directions.

Mila gritted her teeth and slammed her free hand onto the floor, sending a spike of magic and a thought to shape it into the stone. The magic was more than happy to conform to her will; she was, after all, fighting the agents of a tyrant.

The Rougarou was immolated in the name of Mila's

conviction, as a pillar of flame consumed its howling body to ash in seconds.

Mila's shield protected her from the intense heat, but several of the wooden picnic tables burst into flame as the intense heat of her spell washed over them.

Mila dropped her shield and sprinted forward, only to come up short when goblins appeared behind the thralls attacking the Market defenders and stabbed them with knives and spears. They made quick work of the thralls, then sucked in deep breaths to vanish from sight to find their next targets.

A smile spread across Mila's face. Remmy hadn't abandoned her; she had gone for reinforcements. A wash of shame overcame Mila as she realized she had assumed the worst of Remmy, and her smile fell.

In the midst of her turmoil, Mila didn't notice the three small, black, diamond-shaped missiles zip through the smoke roiling off the picnic tables until they slammed into her stomach, blasting her off her feet as they exploded into a shower of black shards.

Several of the slivers sliced into her arms and legs, and two small shards hit her face. One sliced her cheek open and the other ripped through the cartilage of her ear, leaving the top in two ragged pieces.

Yaminah stepped out from behind the burning tables and sneered down at Mila where she lay on her back, trying to figure out what had just happened.

"You're a real problem for me, Mila." Yaminah's sneer twisted into anger.

"Glad I could be of service." Mila felt short of breath

and coughed up a little blood, which she spit at Yaminah's feet.

"I hate the witty ones," the tall woman growled.

She held out a palm towards Mila's chest. "I have to say I'm impressed you survived that first attack. It's usually enough to take anyone out in the first go. Just speaks to your stubborn nature, I suppose. Don't worry, a second round will end your interference quickly enough."

"What the hell are you talking about?" Mila needed to buy a little time. She was faking the pain to keep Yaminah off guard, but Mila knew she had some serious injuries that needed tending to. However, Mila had come to the Market to find out if anyone knew where Azoth might be, and lo and behold his disciple showed up with an army. Maybe she could get the woman to talk before she tried to kill her.

"Azoth is obsessed with you. Somehow you thwarted him, and now he is driven to distraction trying to punish you. It's getting in the way and making him sloppy. I have to do what I can to protect him, and you are currently his biggest threat."

Mila blinked in confusion a few times. "Wow, I didn't think you were going to actually answer that."

Mila saw behind Yaminah that the last of the thralls were going down to goblins. A familiar figure caught her eye as Remmy appeared behind one of the last two Rougarou and sunk two silver daggers into its kidneys. They made eye contact, and Remmy quickly looked at Yaminah's back before giving Mila a nod and sucking in a breath. She vanished as the Rougarou fell to the ground, gouts of blood pouring from the two stab wounds.

Mila focused on Yaminah, who shook with either rage or anticipation, Mila couldn't tell which. "I don't suppose you would tell me where Azoth is right now."

She smiled and took a step backward, her hand wavering slightly. "That would be a little too easy, don't you think, Valkyrie? You have to *earn* a battle with the Lord."

Mila felt like there might be just enough room for her to make a move, but it all depended on how fast Yaminah could get a spell off. That gave Mila an idea.

As she spread her hand out on the floor, Mila quickly channeled magic into another flame spell. This time she focused on making it quick rather than powerful. Mila felt a small drain on her stores of magic as she released her power and intention. A column of fire shot up under Yaminah's feet.

The woman saw it coming from a mile away, of course, and simply stepped back to let the flame jet mere inches from her.

Mila had figured the spell-caster would see it coming, so while she had created the fire spell, she had also boosted her own speed. As soon as the flame jet shot out of the floor, Mila rolled backward onto her feet, yanked the Ivar from its holster, and shot a bolt of raw power into the column of fire as it began to die out.

The fire went out as the small amount of magic ran out, but Yaminah wasn't there.

"I thought you might have been the one, but you were far too obvious," Yaminah breathed into Mila's ear from behind, just before she jammed a short knife into her back and twisted it.

Mila's breath caught in her throat, as the shock of the wound broke through her pain dampening for the briefest of seconds.

"Too bad, really. You were kind of cute for such a self-righteous bit—"

Yaminah's harsh whisper turned to a scream of pain as she shoved Mila forward into a stumbling fall. Mila twisted as she hit the ground and saw the cause of Yaminah's pain. Remmy stood behind her, the two long silver daggers plunged into her back. The blade tips poked out of Yaminah's stomach.

Her scream turned to a snarling growl as she lifted a leg and mule kicked Remmy in the chest, to send her crashing into one of the burning tables, taking the daggers with her.

Remmy rolled out of the fire unscathed but clutched one of her daggers to her chest as she rubbed the spot Yaminah had kicked.

The tall woman stumbled slightly and quickly took stock of the battlefield. There were only two thralls left, and they went down as she watched. Her face hardened as she came to a decision.

With a quick gesture, she opened a black void behind her.

"We shall continue this later, Valkyrie!" She turned and ran through the teleport spell.

Mila ignored her injuries since she had a couple of healing potions and sprinted for the still-open portal. It was her best chance to find Azoth quickly and end this before he became too powerful to do anything about.

From the corner of her eye, she saw Remmy sprinting for her and feared that the goblin would try and stop her.

Mila knew it was a stupid decision to follow Yaminah to an unknown location, but it was the last chance Mila had.

Mila opened her mouth to tell Remmy to back off, but the goblin beat her to it.

"Get the lead out, boss lady! It's going to close!"

Mila blinked in surprise but quickened her step. "I knew I liked you for some reason, Remmy."

"Yeah, you're just as crazy as me."

The goblin woman leaped forward and tackled Mila, giving her just enough forward momentum to take them both into the black void before the portal snapped shut with a sizzling pop.

CHAPTER TEN

Michelle Lister sat behind the counter at Chincoteague Beachwear with the front doors open to let a nice late spring breeze blow through the place.

It was still early for most shoppers, especially since it had been an unusually cold spring, and tourism had been down so far that season, especially for beach activities. The scooter rentals were still strong, but the store itself had been dead since she had started working there for the season.

Michelle pushed her glasses up her nose, turned the page of her Anthropology 333 textbook, put the end of her highlighter in her mouth, and chewed it as she read about the socio-economic ramifications of Genghis Khan's implementation of religious freedom in his empire. It was much more boring than the description led one to expect.

So, when the door darkened with a customer, she took the first chance she had had all day to quit reading the dry text and quickly marked her page, then slid the book onto the counter.

Her jaw dropped open as the largest man she had ever seen in real life entered the store. He didn't have to duck when he came through the door, but it was a close thing. He had a full beard and sharp brown eyes. He sniffed and ran a hand through his slightly shorter than shoulder length hair to reveal an undercut that went all the way around his head.

He spotted her behind the counter and smiled.

She felt her heart flutter at that smile. "Hi. Can I help you find anything?"

He walked over to the counter, slipped a large green hiking pack off his back, and put it on the floor beside the counter. "Hello, Michelle. I'm looking for some beachwear."

Michelle was suddenly suspicious that her friends had sent this guy in to mess with her. How did he know her name? This was probably the work of Ginna. That bitch always... Then she remembered she had a nametag on.

"Um," for some reason, her voice wasn't working properly, "well, you came to the right place."

His good-natured laugh was genuine. "I gathered that from the name." He spotted her textbook and brightened up. "No way! My girlfriend is an anthropologist. Is that what you're studying to be?"

Michelle nodded. "Yeah. I'm in my first year of my master's. Where does your girlfriend work?"

"The Denver Museum of Nature and Science. To be honest, she's been on sabbatical since we met, so I haven't gotten to see her in action yet. She really likes it, though.

Sometimes she gets caught up in some obscure detail in a show we're watching and talks through the whole thing, trying to explain it." He started chuckling. "It's pretty cute."

That sounded annoying to Michelle.

"Yeah. I know what you mean," she lied. "Uh, well, to be honest, we haven't gotten the new shipment of suits in yet this year; it's been a slow start to the season. But if you want to look at what we have left, they're over there. The men's section is from the middle rack all the way to the back."

"Thanks, Michelle. My name's Finn, by the way."

"Nice to meet you, Finn. Let me know if there's anything you need."

"Actually," he lifted the backpack onto the counter, "do you mind if I leave this here while I shop?"

She shook her head. "I don't mind."

"Thanks." He turned and walked down the aisle to the men's section.

Michelle watched him checking sizes, then quickly move down the line.

"Wow, you weren't kidding. It's slim pickings over here." She saw him pull something off the rack and look it over. "These'll work. Do you have a changing room?"

Michelle pointed to the curtained-off rooms at the back of the store. "Back there."

"Thanks. Oh, these look nice." He pulled a pair of leather flip-flops from a rack and took them with him to the changing room.

Michelle went back to reading but couldn't help wondering what Finn looked like without his shirt. He looked pretty cut from what she could see of his fitted black t-shirt. She didn't have to wait long.

"Perfect fit. I'll take them. Oh, and this."

She looked up and began to choke. Finn had changed out of his street clothes and carried them folded up under his arm. He now wore the flip-flops and a black speedo that left nothing to the imagination. He passed by a rack of ladies' hats and found a huge floppy sun yellow hat that he now stretched over his large head. With his chiseled abs and tiny black Speedo, he looked downright scandalous, but as soon as he put on the yellow sun hat, he transformed into something wholesome.

It was confusing. Almost like magic.

Finn stopped at the coolers and picked out a six-pack of craft beer, then grabbed a koozie to go along with them. Once he put everything on the counter, he began to pack it all into his empty backpack.

"What do I owe you?"

Michelle rang it all up, doing her best to not stare. "Um, it'll be a hundred and seventeen fifty."

He handed her two hundreds.

"Keep the change, Michelle." He slung the backpack onto his bare back. "Keep studying. I think you'll like anthropology. The world is a far more mysterious place than you know. Have a good one."

He gave her a friendly wave and a smile, then he was gone.

Michelle stared at the spot he had last been standing in for a full minute before she moved. She finally sat on her stool and shook her head in disbelief.

"Those Speedos were *so* tight!"

Penny fed a small stream of power into the cone-shaped shield she had created to act as a windbreak. It was a pretty simple spell she'd found on a website deep in the dark corners of the web and had adapted to make a cone out of it. So far, she was really happy with its performance.

The thing most people didn't understand about dragons was that there was no limit to how much power they could use in a spell, so long as they had the magic to use. That might not seem like a great advantage, considering most creatures had access to basically unlimited magic, while a dragon's magic was based on how much food they could convert to magical energy. But, like most things in the universe, it was all in how you looked at it.

Right now, Penny was flying across the country, but she didn't want to fly for hours, so she just channeled more power into her flight speed. A Peabrain, for example, if they could fly, would only be able to reach a certain speed, but they could do it forever. Penny, on the other hand, could keep dumping magic into one aspect of her flight, the speed, so she could go as fast as she wanted. While she would eventually run out of magic to use, until then, she could use that power however she chose.

Right now she had chosen to fly at Mach two, which made the cone-shield wonderful since it cut down on her drag and protected her from air friction.

On glancing down, Penny saw the southern shore of Louisiana off in the distance to her right. And the sprawl of New Orleans coming up fast.

Slowing her speed down to something much more

manageable took a few seconds, but once she'd dropped into the sub-five hundred mile-an-hour range, she reached over her shoulder, pulled her new phone from the backpack she had fashioned just to be able to carry it conveniently, and turned it on. She already had the map with the coordinates pulled up and checked it against her position. With a satisfied nod, she put the phone away and flicked her wings into a dive headed for the middle of the bayou.

The ground came up fast as she aimed for an opening between two giant cypress trees. As the canopy shot past in a blur, Penny tilted her wings up and leveled off just a foot above the water in a move that would have made a fighter pilot shit himself with fright.

As she glanced behind her, Penny smiled when she saw how her high-speed passage sucked the water up into a rooster tail that shot into the air about twenty feet or so for a few yards.

She zoomed across the swamp at mind-numbing speeds, until she caught a glimpse of what she was looking for from the corner of her eye. She put on the brakes by flaring her wings and slowed from several hundred miles an hour to a hover in less than a hundred feet.

She scanned the area where she had seen the shimmer. When she squinted just right, she saw it again. She headed in that direction at a much slower pace than before as she looked for signs of any traps or warning alarms. She didn't see anything out of the ordinary.

As she got closer, the shimmer became a dome of weak magical energy. Penny had to admit the spell was impressive. It seemed to be a modified concealment spell that worked much like the artifact she and Finn had used to cloak their old ship, the Anthem. This spell didn't use an artifact but seemed to be powered directly by the lush swamp itself. It was just the kind of thing Penny would have done.

Seeing the imaginative use of magic convinced her that she was on the right track.

At the spell's edge, Penny hesitated, not wanting to disturb the magic and accidentally collapse the spell. After another look, Penny realized the spell was far more robust than she'd initially thought, and she felt confident she could pass through without a problem.

With a deep breath, she moved forward with a flap of her wings. She could feel the static charge of the spell passing over her skin and shivered. As soon as she had passed through the barrier, the empty section of swamp covered by the dome was suddenly not empty.

Under the dome, two huge cypress trees towered a hundred feet into the air with trunks ten or twelve feet across at the base. While the trees were impressive on their own, the house built into their branches struck Penny as the true marvel.

The house might only be one story tall, but it had been built between and around the trunks to cover thousands of square feet. It hung about fifty feet above the swamp, on which a small boathouse and dock floated, a simple dingy tied to the dock.

The house itself had been made of glass and steel and looked like something that should be in downtown Singapore rather than in the bayous of Louisiana. A wide deck jutted out from the house on all sides, providing additional floor space filled with lawn furniture in clustered groups.

The most amazing thing about the deck was that a full-sized pool had been built into it and filled to the brim with crystal clear water, but when Penny looked below the deck, the part where the tank should be showing didn't exist.

If the giant concealment spell weren't a sure giveaway, then the magical swimming pool was proof enough that this was not just some eccentric billionaire's house.

Penny slowly circled the house from above just to take it all in before she went in for introductions.

Beside the pool, reclining on a lounge chair, Penny spotted a tall, slender woman in a white bikini and large black sunglasses. Her pixie-cut hair had been dyed a vibrant blue that matched her finger and toenail polish.

As Penny circled closer, she saw that the woman had a tattoo just below her belly button that Penny recognized as the crest of the Breck family. This was the right place.

On deciding just get it over with, Penny dropped the last dozen feet and landed on the deck rail on the opposite side of the pool from the woman.

The entire side of the house had glass doors that folded open so that interior and the deck were all one space. Penny spotted a slightly pudgy man with curly blond hair wearing a pink Henley and khaki cargo shorts sitting inside at a white marble kitchen island. He worked on a laptop, tapping at the keys at an impressive rate.

With the large sunglasses, Penny couldn't tell if the woman was asleep or not. Just as Penny was about to fly closer, the woman spoke.

"Well, now. What are the chances that a faerie dragon just decides to land on my balcony?" Her tone was humorous, but she didn't smile.

Penny cleared her throat, nervous for the first time in a long time. "Shir shee, shee? *I don't suppose you understand draconic?*"

The woman sat up and finally smiled. "What kind of historical artificer doesn't speak draconic? Most of the good stuff was made by your people."

Penny sagged in relief. She hated having to find ways to communicate when she was trying to do complicated work.

"Squee! Chi chi, shir? *Thank the turds of Geralt. I figured if anyone spoke it, it would be you. My name is Penny, and I'm hoping you might be able to help me solve a problem. Just so we're on the same page, you are Rebecca Breck, right?*"

"I am." She rose and wrapped a long white sarong around her waist. "I thought all the faerie dragons on Earth were dead?"

Penny smiled and spread her arms, as if to say, "Obviously not."

"What?" the blond man called out from the kitchen.

"Nothing, honey. Why don't you come out here for a second? There's someone you should meet."

The man slipped off the stool and added a few words to whatever he was working on, then dragged himself away and came outside, squinting against the bright sun. As he stepped up next to Rebecca, it became apparent that he was a good five inches shorter than her.

"What are you saying, honey?"

"Lance, this is Penny. Penny, this is my husband Lance."

"Chi chi. Shir squee. *A pleasure, Lance. Can you tell him I really like the house? This place is a real work of art.*"

"I understand you." Lance laughed. "Thanks, we worked

hard on it. The pool was my idea." He puffed up at that a little.

A small, curly-haired child about four or five years old ran out of the house and wrapped his arms around Rebecca's legs, hiding from Penny's view as best he could. His hair might be blond like Lance's, but the little guy looked thin and gangly like Penny imagined Rebecca must've been as a child.

"This is our son Grimmly." Rebecca squatted and put a hand on his back to reassure him. "Grimm, this is Penny. She needs our help. What do you think; should we help her?"

Grimm nodded vigorously. "Yeah!"

"That's right. If people ask for help, then you should at least try." Rebecca rubbed the child's back affectionately but smiled up at Penny. "So, what is this thing that you need our help with?"

"Squee shir. *I need to figure out how to kill a Drude.*"

Lance barked a laugh. "Oh, is that all?"

Penny nodded.

Lance's face fell. "Seriously?"

Penny nodded.

"Shit."

"Shit!" Grimm parroted in a loud shout.

"You said it, buddy."

CHAPTER ELEVEN

Mila and Remmy fell for far too long, considering how high off the ground they had been when they entered the portal—hardly more than a foot. Mila hoped it was an effect of the portal and not an indication that they had somehow entered a place in between realities and become stuck there.

Just as Mila's concern began to rise to alarm, the world materialized around her and Remmy, and they fell the rest of the way to the ground in a pile of tangled limbs.

Remmy scrambled to her feet and took a defensive stance, then drew two long silver daggers from matching sheaths hanging from a dark brown leather belt slung low on her hips. She had discarded her hoodie before joining the fight, but Mila could see that she had tucked her phone into her waistband at the small of her back.

Mila got to her feet more slowly. The pain of her injuries was still blocked, but a very large portion of her power seemed to be flowing into her body in a way she didn't quite understand. Not to mention, she felt woozy from the blood loss from being stabbed in the kidney.

As she stumbled forward, Mila caught herself on a huge machine with flaking green paint. She blinked as she tried to figure out where they were, but she couldn't focus. There was a smell like oil and steel, along with a hint of rotting wood. The most prevalent smell was that of the ocean.

The room they'd landed in felt large, but she couldn't be sure because it was dark and old factory machines years out of date and half covered in rust surrounded them. They seemed to be tucked away in a corner of an old factory or warehouse.

Mila screwed her eyes shut and traced the line of magic being sucked away at such a high rate. From the source, an area at the back of her skull, Mila followed the line of power as it twisted through her. The magic spiraling down her spine flowed to the small of her back, then branched off to disappear into the stab wound Yaminah had given her.

Remmy gently placed her hand on Mila's side as she leaned on the old machinery. "You need to take a healin' potion, boss lady. You lost a lotta blood. Let me take a look at the wound."

Mila nodded, and Remmy helped her get the shredded hoodie off. She felt warm hands on her back lift her gray t-shirt gently.

"How the hell did she get through the mythril?" Mila hissed, short on breath and woozy at the constant drain on her magic.

"Holy shit, boss. This looks insane. There's a residue of

magic on the mythril, but the wound is closing up on its own." Remmy grabbed the discarded hoodie and used it as a rag to clear the blood from the wound to see what was happening better. "Yeah, you're healing this thing up pretty good. How are you doin' that?"

Mila shook her head. "I don't know, but it's taking a huge amount of power."

"There it goes. Just closed up, looks as good as new." Remmy frowned when she saw Mila still leaned on the machine, her eyes closed tight. "You get stabbed somewhere else?"

Mila shook her head. "Broken rib."

As she said it, she heard an audible pop from inside her chest cavity as the bone reset.

A few seconds later, the drain stopped, and Mila took a deep breath. She finally felt like herself.

She straightened and ran a hand over the stab wound but felt nothing other than a bit of residual blood becoming tacky as it dried. The edges of the mythril chainmail were cleanly cut, and as she ran her hand over them, they reconnected, one tiny link at a time. The armor seemed to be able to heal on its own, which was good, Mila thought, because she didn't feel like she had much left in the tank.

"You all good?" Remmy asked softly.

Mila nodded. "Yeah, I'm good. Did you see where Yaminah went?"

"Up the stairs. Probably through that door." Remmy pointed to a set of iron mesh stairs that led up to a walkway. A metal door had been set into a sheet metal wall beside the catwalk.

Mila looked up. Sure enough, they stood in a large factory of some kind. The roof towered overhead and had an intricate set of track beams with old winch cranes dangling from them. Windows lined the walls close to the ceiling, letting in only a small amount of light through the built-up grime on the glass.

"Did you see her go in there?" Mila picked up Gram from the floor where she had dropped it when they'd landed.

"Nope. She was already gone when we came through. Otherwise, we would be in the middle of a fight that we probably wouldn't be winning. I can definitely smell a bunch of Rougarou somewhere in here."

Mila took a sniff but didn't detect anything new on the air. "How can you smell them? All I smell is oil and steel."

Remmy sniffed again. "It kinda smells like rotting wood and sweat with a dash of copper thrown in. How can you not smell that?"

Mila took another sniff and did smell the rotting wood, but she had thought it was just rotting wood. Now that she looked around, she decided she'd be surprised if there was any wood in the building at all, let alone enough to fill the building with the smell of rot.

"I can smell it," Mila said, taking another sniff. "I just thought that was wood rot. I guess it would help to know what things smell like if I want to identify them that way. So how did you know Yaminah went up the stairs?"

Remmy pointed at the floor. "Blood trail. I had both my daggers in, and she's leakin' like a government scandal."

Mila had missed it at first due to the dim lighting and the grimy concrete floor, but Remmy was right. A trail of blood droplets led from the corner they stood in right to the stairs. Mila even spotted some wet spots on the steps as they reflected what little light there was.

Mila pulled out the Ivar and unlocked the safety. "Let's go. We need to find out where we are and call for some reinforcements. We need to stay quiet. I think you're right; we would be overrun in here."

Mila took the lead as they climbed the stairs, her gun held in both hands close to her face. She had to be careful to place her feet softly, or the iron mesh would ring out. Remmy, on the other hand, seemed to have no problem at all staying silent, which Mila figured had to be a part of her magic.

At the top of the stairs, Mila checked that the walkway was clear and noticed a heavy metal door at the far end that likely led to an outside stairway. Mila noted it just in case they had to make a quick exit, then padded softly to the other steel door Remmy had pointed out a few strides down the catwalk.

"Good guess on her coming this way." Mila pointed out the smeared blood on the flaking blue paint next to the silver doorknob.

Remmy placed an ear to the door and listened for a full thirty seconds before she straightened and nodded. "I think it's clear."

Mila nodded back, then gripped the knob carefully as she held the Ivar so that it would point into the room as soon as she opened the door. "Ready?"

Remmy nodded. Mila turned the knob, shoved the door open sharply, and bounced in, gun first, to give Remmy room to come in behind her.

The room was dark except for a row of large windows on the far side of the large space that overlooked the factory floor and let in some of the dingy light. However, a dozen rows of metal shelving blocked most of that light. A walkway passed through the center of the rows, but the rest of the room was blocked from view.

Mila swallowed hard, then quietly began to move forward, Remmy a step or two behind her, blades out and ready to strike.

Mila stepped into the first aisle, the Ivar pointed down its length, and nearly pulled the trigger out of shock.

A dozen slack-jawed people stood packed together, staring her way blankly.

Mila spun around and saw a similar number of thralls on the other side. Not one of them seemed to notice she was there.

"Fucking hell," Mila whispered as she let out a pent-up breath. "I nearly shit myself right there."

There was no answer, and Mila quickly looked around for Remmy. The goblin stood on the other side of the room beside the windows.

"There's more in each row, but they aren't moving either."

Mila nodded and quickly made her way to Remmy, making a mental tally as she glanced down each row. She knelt down beside Remmy so she couldn't be seen through the windows from below.

"There are at least a dozen thralls on each side in every row," Mila whispered. "That's like three hundred thralls. How the fuck has Azoth built up numbers like this without anyone noticing. He must be taking dozens every day, and that's not even mentioning all the people he changes into Rougarou. If a dozen people vanished in one city, there would be a national emergency."

Remmy snorted. "I'm guessing most of these people are coming from places that aren't exactly civilian conscious. And if you think you couldn't take a few dozen homeless people from a city without raising much suspicion, then you are much more sheltered than I thought, boss lady. There are forgotten people all over the world if you take the time to look for them."

Mila frowned, but Remmy was right. She hadn't been thinking about those unfortunate enough that they slipped under the radar. "You're right; I am naive. But it still begs the question of how he is rounding them up. He can't very well send out a pack of thralls; they look like shambling zombies. And the Rougarou are out of the question. Plus, it must take a considerable amount of magic to make this many thralls. The one time I saw him make a Rougarou, it looked like it took a lot of power to change that poor elf woman."

"I would bet that it does take more power to convert magicals, but I don't think most of the thralls are magicals. I think they're just Peabrains. He wouldn't get much power out of them, but it probably doesn't take much to enslave them either."

The sound of shouting out in the factory caught their attention. Mila stood slightly to see what was going on, but there was a walkway that blocked her view. She saw a door in the corner of the room that led out onto the catwalk. Quickly squat-running over to the metal door, she gently opened it and slipped out onto the walkway, Remmy right behind her.

Mila peered through the railing and saw Azoth standing in the middle of a large cleared-out area of floor just below them. He held Yaminah up by the throat with one of the smoke tentacles he had used to restrain Finn.

Yaminah's body hung three feet off the ground as she tried to pry the tentacle loose with her fingers. Mila could see that the stab wounds Remmy had inflicted were still dripping blood, creating a small pool under Yaminah's twitching feet.

"Why would you go after her?" Azoth roared, his normally creaking voice sounding more like metal sheets being ripped in half. "You know I am saving her for last. Now she knows we can get to her, and she will flee."

"I was only trying to protect you." Yaminah choked out. "My Geas won't let me act against you. That means there is truth in me saying that your obsession with her is harmful to your greater goal."

That gave Azoth pause, and the tentacle pulled her close to swirling void where his face should have been. "Swear to me that you are not trying to thwart me. You have good ideas. I would hate to have to dispose of you for something as simple as rebellion."

"I swear it. I can't. The Geas would kill me on the spot."

Azoth considered Yaminah for a long breath, then unraveled the tentacle and dropped her in a heap at his feet to cough and suck in deep breaths.

"I will return shortly. Another Lone Valkyrie is ready for me to pluck from its den." His tentacle withdrew under the edge of his gray robe.

Mila's eyes went wide. She had assumed Azoth had normal legs under that robe, but it appeared he also had tentacles, or maybe *just* tentacles. She should probably find out what a Drude actually looked like. Up until that moment, she had assumed he was humanoid, but there was no reason that he had to be. For all she knew, he could be a pile of sentient octopuses, or three children standing on each other's shoulders...with a trained octopus.

"Azoth, you must be careful," Yaminah pleaded, slowly regaining her feet. "Capturing *that* one was pure luck," she said, pointing off in a direction Mila couldn't see. "It only worked because she had become weak while she was in close proximity to her exiled sister."

"Do not question my strength!" Azoth roared.

"I was merely advising caution for your own wellbeing." Yaminah didn't back down from the obviously irritated Drude, which impressed Mila quite a bit, even if she was a murderous psychopath.

Mila slowly crouch-walked along the walkway, trying to get to an angle where she could see who Yaminah had been pointing at. Hopefully, it was her sister from Dubai, and she could save her, or at the very least, kill her to save her soul for another life and deny Azoth the pleasure.

"You have done well in organizing my army and finding me so many to convert, but do not think to overstep your place. I own you. You serve me. Do not presume to act on my behalf without my knowledge."

Yaminah bowed her head and nodded. "I will do my best."

Azoth flicked his hand in the air, and a void portal

ripped opened behind him. "See that your best is good enough."

Mila came to the exterior wall of the factory where the catwalk turned ninety degrees to follow along it the entire length of the building. She turned and finally got an angle to see who they were talking about.

Two sets of the magic-canceling restraints like those Mila had seen the Drude use in the past shackled the Valkyrie. As with Heather, the restraints were attached to a long chain that had been hung from one of the many cranes suspended from the ceiling. The woman had been hoisted a foot off the ground, so the shackles held her entire weight.

Mila winced when she saw the woman's hands had turned purple from her time hanging there. Though she wanted nothing more than to run down and free the woman from her painful ordeal, Mila restrained herself because it would be a suicide run.

With her head down and her long dark hair hanging in her face, Mila found it impossible to identify the Valkyrie for certain, but there seemed to be something familiar about her. She wore a white blouse that had been torn in a struggle. Several blood stains had soaked into the white material, but they had all turned a ruddy brown color to show the wounds had stopped bleeding. She had on one black stiletto heel, with the other nowhere to be seen. A tight khaki pencil skirt finished off a very business-oriented outfit.

Mila's eyes widened.

"That's Victoria," she whispered to Remmy. "How the fuck was he able to catch her?"

Remmy gave her a shrug. "No one's invulnerable."

Azoth turned back to Yaminah. "If she tries anything when she wakes, I want you to hurt her until she stops, do you understand me?"

Yaminah nodded. "I understand."

"Good. I will return in a few hours. Perhaps you can refrain from running off on some crusade this time."

Yaminah didn't say anything but kept her head bowed in deference.

Azoth turned and stepped through the portal, which slammed shut with a snapping sound.

"We need to get out of here, and get word to the sisterhood," Mila whispered, indicating that Remmy should start heading back the way they had come.

After two steps, the Valkyrie phone in her pocket vibrated, followed by a ringing that echoed off the steel walls.

Mila's heart spiked as she pulled the phone out and mashed her fingers onto the screen, silencing it. It was far too late, though.

When Mila looked back over the rail, Yaminah was nowhere to be seen.

"Run!" Mila barked, but Remmy was one step ahead of her and already making the turn on the catwalk.

CHAPTER TWELVE

Remmy sprinted down the catwalk, Mila hot on her heels.

"Back through the room we just came out of!" Mila waved at the still-open door. "There was an exit on the first catwalk!"

Remmy nodded and grabbed the frame of the door, using it as a pivot and rounded the doorway without slowing down. They ran down the middle aisle, arms pumping.

Movement caught Mila's attention. She glanced to the side just as three thralls dove for her. Mila shouted in surprise, then instinctively aimed the Ivar and pulled the trigger.

The dark room lit up as if lightning had struck as the magical bolt ripped through the three thralls and exploded when it hit the metal shelf beside them.

Mila and Remmy flew through the air toward the far end of the room as the shock wave blasted them off their feet. A crashing sound followed by a second broke through the ringing in Mila's ears. As she hit the floor, tucked her shoulder, and rolled back onto her feet, she saw that the shelves had tipped and now knocked over the ones beside them in a domino effect.

They didn't have time to watch the chaos as thralls poured out of the aisles and stumbled towards them. Thralls even crawled out of the spaces between the fallen shelves.

Remmy grabbed Mila's hand and pulled her toward the door. "Come on, boss! No time to gawk!"

Mila ran for the doorway. Luckily they had left it open when they first entered, so they didn't have to take precious seconds to open it. Mila grabbed the handle and yanked it shut as they passed through, slamming the heavy metal into the frame. She looked frantically for a lock, but this was the outside of the door, so she was SOL.

On instinct, Mila channeled magic into the metal of the door through the handle. The draw on her already limited magical reserves drained her even more, but the door heated up at an exponential rate. In seconds, the flaking paint smoked and bubbled, and the metal underneath glowed cherry red.

Mila pulled hard, warping the metal slab and mashing the now soft metal of the door into the frame. As she withdrew her magic and its effects, the soft metal hardened as it cooled, the door welded to the frame.

She jumped back when thralls slammed into it and began pounding on it as they tried to get through.

"Dude, that was sweet!" Remmy shouted in surprise.

Mila pointed to the door at the end of the catwalk. "There."

A small purplish black lightning bolt sizzled past Mila's face, missed her blood-encrusted jaw by inches, and slammed into the wall. The metal wall rang with the impact as a hole the size of Mila's fist appeared with glowing orange edges where the metal had melted away.

Mila spun and saw Yaminah at the far end of the catwalk where the interior of the building they had just run through ended. She chugged a healing potion and aimed a finger Mila's way.

Another witch bolt shot from her extended finger, and Mila deflected it with a hastily formed shield. The bolt slammed into the door she had just welded shut and blasted a hole in the top corner. Immediately a dozen hands gripped the still-hot metal and pulled hard to rip apart the welded surfaces with a loud screech.

The sound of scrambling claws on steel yanked Mila's attention back to Yaminah just as a dozen Rougarou charged around the corner at full speed past the still-healing woman.

"Go! Go! Go!" Mila ran for the exit. She prayed the door wasn't locked, then aimed the Ivar at the handle and shot.

The celestial bolt blasted the handle, disintegrating it and the lock in one go, and slammed the door wide open.

Remmy burst through the opening and leaped over the rail of the stairway that led to the ground. Mila vaulted the rail with one hand, half-blinded by the bright light of day.

She hit the pavement right behind Remmy who sprinted for the chain-link fence that surrounded the property. Mila ran after her, using a bit of magic to help her speed up. As she passed Remmy, Mila slammed her hand against the fence links and quickly channeled more magic into them. A four-foot circle of the metal wires instantly turned to liquid and dropped to the ground with a series of splattering sounds.

Still at a full run, Remmy hopped through the hole with Mila right behind her.

They had crossed into a large dock operation, with thousands of shipping containers stacked four or five high in neat rows. Remmy aimed for the closest stack and didn't stop running until she hid behind the bottom-most orange metal container.

Mila slid to a stop beside the goblin and leaned around the corner of the container.

Yaminah stood on the platform at the top of the stairs, her face sour and her fists clenched. They made eye contact for a few seconds before Yaminah turned, pulled the door closed behind her, and returned to her lair.

Mila breathed a sigh of relief, slamming her back against the container and sliding down to sit on her butt. She wrapped her arms around her legs and put her forehead on her knees while she caught her breath.

"That was exciting," Remmy said with enthusiasm.

Mila snorted. "Yeah, it was a real butt clencher. Too bad we need to go back soon."

Remmy nodded as she pulled her phone out from her waistband and unlocked it. "We should probably get some help for that. It was fun the first time, but it's going to suck if they know we're coming."

"Agreed."

"Hey!" A male voice rang out not far away.

Mila looked up in surprise and saw an overweight man

in a hard hat and a vest walking toward them, a clipboard in one hand.

Mila quickly put the Ivar back in its holster, then stood up and stepped out of the shadow of the stacked containers. She glanced back, but Remmy was nowhere to be seen.

The man's expression went from angry to shocked to concerned in the blink of an eye as he took in her shredded hoodie and bloody face and hands.

"Are you okay, little lady?"

Mila realized what she must look like and thought fast. She smiled and nodded. "Yeah, I'm fine. This is just makeup…for a movie we're shooting. Down the street."

He looked doubtful. "A movie?"

"It's a horror movie?" Mila suggested.

The man frowned, but could obviously tell that she was fine, despite the grisly look of her. "Well, I don't really care why you look like you just jumped through a woodchipper; you can't be here. This is a shipping port. How the hell did you even get on the property?"

Remmy appeared behind the man, exhaling as quietly as she could as she leaned against a container with one hand, fanned her face with the other, then sucked in a quiet lungful of air.

"Oh, I got lost looking for the set." She pointed towards the fence with the hole in it and continued in as innocent a voice as she could muster. "I came across a hole in the fence and headed over here. If only authorized personnel are allowed on the premises, you should close up that hole."

The man looked towards the fence with concern, then his eyes went wide. "Holy shit. That's a big hole. Right, you come with me. I'll escort you off the property."

As the man turned, Remmy sucked in another breath and vanished before he caught a glimpse of her.

Mila chuckled at the goblin's great efforts not to be seen. While her actions might be admirable, they were completely unnecessary. It seemed Remmy had completely forgotten that her concealment spell was still active.

As they followed the man through the enormous ship-yard, Mila looked for clues as to where they actually were, but all she could tell was that there was water and the weather, while a little chilly, wasn't all that bad. Then they came around a row of stacked containers, and Mila knew exactly where they were.

In the distance, the unmistakable lines of the Golden Gate Bridge spanned the large bay that fed the shipyard.

San Francisco, California. She had never been to the city before, but anyone who watched even a little television knew what the Golden Gate Bridge looked like.

Along the way, Remmy would appear in a shadowed corner to catch her breath, then vanish again after an exaggerated inhale only to pop up half a minute later in a different location.

The man led Mila to a gated entrance with several guards packed into a tiny glass booth that checked every vehicle in and out. Beside the barricades was a gate for foot traffic, and the man opened it and used his clipboard to wave her through.

"Thanks for letting me know about the hole in the fence. We'll have it fixed within the hour, so don't even think about sneaking in here again." His stern face came back as he stared down at Mila as if she were lucky he was so kind.

Given what little she knew about the shipping industry and their regulation by the government, she decided he might very well be doing her a favor. "Thank you, good sir. I'm just glad you found me and showed me the way out."

She walked through the gate and headed down the sidewalk in what she hoped was the opposite direction from the old factory Azoth was using. The walk out had taken several turns through the maze of containers, and she wasn't sure where she was.

After walking the several hundred yards down the street it took to pass the truck and rail entrances to the shipyard, Mila finally came upon some buildings lining the street. She ducked into the first alley she came to and found Remmy waiting for her, huffing deep breaths.

"You know you still have your concealment spell on, right? You could have just walked out with me. We could have told the guy you were my little sister or something," Mila said with a smile at the puffing goblin.

Remmy's eyes opened wide. "Oh, yeah! I totally forgot about that. Oh, well. I needed the practice. So what now, boss?"

"Now I need to call in the cavalry," she said, pulling the Valkyrie phone from her pocket. "Then we need to find some clothes that aren't either shredded or covered in blood. You think you can use your phone to find us a thrift store or something?"

Remmy nodded. "That's what I was doing when the fat guy came over. I'll find us something close."

Mila nodded and went to turn on the phone but saw that it was already connected to someone. She must have answered the phone when it went off in the factory instead of silencing it.

Holding the phone up to her ear, Mila couldn't hear anything, but it was connected to a call.

"Hello?"

The phone must have been on mute because Mila had to quickly pull the speaker away from her ear as a roaring noise of wind suddenly blasted from the other end of the call.

"Mila!" Missy shouted through the receiver. "What the hell are you doing over there? It sounded like you were just in the middle of a fight."

"Missy! We have a huge problem."

"Tell me about it. There's a Drude stealing our sisters out from under us. And to top it all off, Victoria isn't answering my calls. That's why I rang you. Have you talked to her since this morning?"

"Funny you should mention that."

CHAPTER THIRTEEN

Mila explained the last half-hour to Missy as quickly as she could, starting at the Market and ending with their run from Yaminah and Azoth's minions.

"We need to get the rest of the Valkyries out looking for his next victim," Mila said with conviction. "It sounded like he already knew where she was located, so time is of the essence. If we can get eyes on all the Lone Valkyries, then we will catch him alone, without his army to back him up. We could end this right now."

The wind noise on Missy's side of the call was distracting and made the eldest Valkyrie have to shout to be heard. "I'm on my way to one of the lone sisters now, and the others have sisters either headed their way or already close by. When he shows up, we'll know. Everyone has been alerted to send a message as soon as anything happens. I need you to stay close by the abandoned factory and let us know if anyone tries to leave. Once we take care of Azoth, then we can free Victoria. Being close by will drain you and Victoria's power, so don't be alarmed when you feel the effects. It'll be fine. You won't need to fight, and I can call when we're arriving to warn you away, so your presence doesn't affect the rest of the sisters. You did great work, but please don't go jumping through portals to unknown locations again. You got lucky this time."

Mila frowned. "You just want me to stand around keeping watch? I should go in and get Victoria while you're keeping Azoth busy. This might be the best chance to save her. What if he gets away from you and comes back? We can't fight Azoth and his minions; there are way too many of them."

"No!" Missy shouted, a little too loudly, making Mila have to pull the phone away for a second. "Don't go in there alone. Victoria will be fine. You would just be throwing your life away. It's impossible, besides the drain on your magic being that close to Victoria has to already be affecting you. Every minute you two are close, you'll just get weaker. Forget about Victoria, and just stay close by, watching for anything out of the ordinary. I'll call you when we have taken care of Azoth. I have to go, I'm here. Remember, don't go in for a rescue mission; you're not ready for something like that."

Mila gritted her teeth. "You got it, Missy. I'll just keep watch."

"Good." Missy sighed with relief. "Talk with you soon."

Mila stabbed the end call button hard enough that she nearly broke her finger. Why did everyone underestimate her? The corner of her mouth went up when she realized that wasn't true. Finn didn't underestimate her. Hell, most of the time he even warned people ahead of time that she was going to kick their ass, and they still didn't believe it.

That got her thinking like a dwarf. What would Finn do? Sit tight and keep watch? Fuck no. He would charge in, his berserker rage whipped into a frenzy, and start chopping people in half. While that sounded appealing, it also sounded like something she would have to call plan C. She wasn't exactly the front-line brute force kind of weapon. She wasn't even the knife-in-the-back kind of weapon. No, she decided she was more the twist your disadvantages into advantages kind of weapon. The kind the enemy didn't expect.

The problem was that this whole thing wasn't adding up. On the surface, she could see how they had gotten here with Azoth and the Valkyries being hunted down one by one, but when she really started examining the situation, it seemed like there was a third player working in the background. Mila suspected it was Yaminah. That woman was defiant and wickedly smart, only giving Azoth the bare minimum of obedience. Mila suspected she was orchestrating a lot more behind the scenes than Azoth realized. Mila just needed to figure out how and why. What did she stand to gain by making Azoth so powerful?

"So, we have watch duty, huh?" Remmy looked up from her phone.

"No," Mila replied, her eyes narrowed in deep thought.

After a moment, she shook off her contemplative mood and smiled down at the tan-skinned Remmy. "No, we are not going to stand by and watch. We're going to rescue Victoria, but there are a few things we need to do before that. Did you find anywhere we can get cleaned up and some new clothes?"

Mila closed her eyes and sighed as she remembered something. "Fuck. I don't have my wallet or my phone. I can't pay for anything."

Remmy reached into her black sports bra and pulled out her roll of cash. "Don't worry. I have us covered."

"Thank fuck. Where did you get that much cash anyway? I meant to ask when you bought lunch, but we were interrupted by Braid Girl back there." She hiked a thumb in the direction she thought Yaminah most likely was. "Did you get a job I don't know about?"

Remmy started searching along the side of the old brick building in the alley. "No, I can't get a job out there with the Peabrains; they all think I'm a kid or a freak. I wouldn't want to do some borin' job anyway; I'm a warrior. Ah, found one. Come over here." Remmy began rummaging through a trashcan, tossing out an old coffee filter and a bag of onions that had green shoots two feet long sticking out of them, before her face brightened and she pulled out several crumpled-up newspapers. "This'll work."

Mila walked over to Remmy and saw a water spigot without a handle in the wall beside a metal door that had Furmin & Shuke Attorneys at Law: Package Delivery written on it.

"I guess you could say I work for Finn mostly. He has me run errands for him, and he pays me in cash. He always gives me way too much, and I try to tell him so, but he doesn't believe me. That guy doesn't get money at all." Remmy stacked the papers on a trashcan lid, bent over the spigot, stuck her finger into the square socket where a handle key would normally fit, and twisted. A blast of murky water coughed out of the spigot a couple of times before it started to flow at a steady rate. After a few seconds, the murky water turned clear as the sediment in the pipes was washed out.

"He understands money. He just acts like he doesn't so he can overpay people and get away with it. He wants you to have it. Uh, what are you doing?" Mila cocked her head to one side as she tried to figure out if Remmy was thirsty or if she just wanted to mess with a couple of lawyers' water bill by leaving the spigot running. It wasn't a bad prank, but hardly the time for it.

Remmy gave her a once over. "I'm not exactly sure what I look like right now, but if you're any indication, I must look like I just chopped twenty people up with an axe and rolled around in the gore for ten minutes." She undid her holster and gently placed the two daggers and belt on the trashcan lid beside the newspapers. Then, in one quick motion, she pulled her blood-soaked sports bra off and began rinsing it in the water. "We need to clean up a little if we're going to be walking out in the open. I know this is San Francisco, but even they have a line we can't cross."

Mila blushed and quickly looked around to see if anyone was watching, but it was still relatively early in the day, and most people were just settling in to work, leaving the streets mostly empty. When she turned back, her eyes bugged out a little at the sight of Remmy, now pantless, scrubbing the blood from her body with her wadded-up shorts.

"Come on, Mila. Get in here. You look like a blood ghost."

Mila knew Remmy was right. She couldn't very well walk the streets looking like a mobile murder scene, but she wasn't quite as free-spirited as the little goblin. Rolling a dumpster away from the wall, she created at least a little nook where they could wash in relative privacy, but if anyone happened to walk down the alley or look out one of the windows, they were going to get a show.

Reluctantly, Mila undid her corset and laid it on the ground. With a deep breath to steady herself for her first round of public nudity, she pulled her t-shirt off, followed by her sports bra. Halfway there, she powered through and had her shoes and pants off in one go.

"Feels good, huh?" Remmy said with a knowing nod at her naked body.

"You are a strange goblin, Remmy. But I have to say you are resourceful." Mila used her black leggings as a sponge to clean the blood from her face. "Speaking of, did you find somewhere close by we can get some clothes?"

"Yeah, I have just the place. It's about a mile away, but it'll be worth the walk. My cousin works there. He can hook us up big time."

"What's it called?"

Remmy smiled. "It's a surprise. You'll love it."

Mila looked down and felt a chill run through her as she saw the river of red-stained water flowing from her.

"I really wish Penny were here."

"To fight with us?" Remmy scrubbed her armpit.

"No. So she could use her cleansing spell on us."

Remmy's mouth dropped open. "And miss a chance to be naked?"

"You are *so* weird," Mila laughed.

Remmy dropped her makeshift rag and stood to perform a full-body flex, like a fitness model in miniature. "It's a crime not to break this thing out as much as I can."

Mila laughed and shook her head in amused disbelief.

CHAPTER FOURTEEN

Finn smiled and tipped his enormous yellow sun hat as he walked past two middle-aged women reclining on their towels and staring with slack-jawed confusion.

Finn was having the time of his life. The fresh ocean air felt invigorating, and walking down the beach fighting the sand was great exercise. Aside from all the stares he was getting, it was a perfect way to spend a morning.

He wasn't sure why he was getting so many stares, but he suspected it was jealousy over his amazing new hat.

The flip-flops were wonderful for the long walk on the asphalt to get to the beach, but as soon as he was in the sand, he stowed them in his pack so he could feel the warm sand granules between his toes.

He took a sip from his second craft beer, stuffed in the pink koozie, and smacked his lips. It was a local brew from Black Narrows Brewing Company, which was located on the island, at least according to what the can said. He was thoroughly enjoying it. It was called Chincoteague Salts, described as a tart oyster wheat. It was a slightly hazy wheat beer with an aftertaste that reminded him of all the best parts of the ocean. He thought it had just the right amount of weird that Mila would love it, and decided to save a couple of cans for her.

He reached down to adjust the black speedo for the tenth time. It wasn't that the tight little swim trunks weren't comfortable, quite the opposite actually. As soon as he had tried them on, he knew there was no other swimwear he would even consider. He felt like he was wearing nothing at all, the way swimming should feel.

As a child, he had gone swimming many times at school and with his caretakers at his father's palace, and not once had he ever seen anything even resembling swimwear for men or women. Every dwarf swam in the nude. There was just something amazing about jumping into the freezing waters, naked and alone, to battle hypothermia with nothing but your strength of will. Maybe it was just a dwarf thing.

The reason he kept having to make adjustments was that while wearing the Speedo, he didn't have a way to attach his weapon harness. However, he didn't want to have to rummage through the pack if he needed a weapon quickly, so he made a compromise.

Fragar folded down into its handle was only about six inches long and an inch thick. He found that with a little personal adjusting, he was able to store the handle down the front of his trunks without it showing due to the trunk's other occupants. It was the best solution he could come up with to get to the weapon fast but also keep it securely on his person. He thought of it as an elegant solution to a mundane problem.

The issue was that as he walked, the handle would work itself into an awkward position, making a quick draw of the weapon not only impossible but posing serious danger to his man-bits.

"Jesus, dude. Nice banana hammock. Looks like you're smuggling an axe handle in there!"

Finn looked at a group of laughing college-age men and women sitting in folding beach chairs or lying out on large towels. They had gathered around a huge cooler packed with cheap beers and what looked like premixed margaritas. Several large umbrellas kept most of the sun off them. They looked like they were ready for a long day of drinking and soaking up the sun.

A large guy laughed at his own observation, egged on by the rest of the group. Close beside him sat a young woman who leered very obviously at Finn's body as she bit her bottom lip.

The look reminded Finn of the time he had been stared down by one of the apex predators out on the Gomina Savanna. He hoped the young woman wouldn't charge him like the Sabertoothed Hellcat had. He still had a scar on his left butt cheek from that encounter.

Finn looked down at the bulging front of his speedo, but couldn't see the handle at all. "You can see that?"

"Oh, yeah. I can see it," The woman purred, making the guy snap his head her way in surprise as the rest of the group burst out in a new round of laughter.

"Dammit! I thought I had it tucked in just right," Finn

said, trying to adjust again, but not seeing where Fragar was pressed against the material.

"You most definitely do, big guy. It's perfect!" Another girl lying on a beach towel gave Finn a thumbs-up as she took a swig of her margarita.

"Wait, so you can't see the axe handle anymore?" Finn asked, confused.

One of the guys in the back burst into laughter. "Dude, are you fucking with us?"

"Not at all." Finn walked over to the group, maybe they were having a hard time spotting it from that distance. "I thought I had the handle hidden pretty well."

"Oh, my God," the guy in the chair said in disgust. The joke had gone too far in his mind now that he was staring down Finn's bulging speedo. "You call it 'the Handle?'"

Finn laughed. "Well, that's the best thing to call it. Technically speaking, the handle is much larger when it unfolds. Right now, I guess it's more of an axe *grip*, but calling it a grip is ridiculous."

"What the fuck, dude?" the guy asked.

The girl's eyes got wide and she said, "It gets *bigger*?"

Finn laughed. "Of course it does. It wouldn't be much of a weapon if it didn't."

"That's hot." The girl on the towel said matter-of-factly.

"Well, if you can see it, then maybe I should just take it out." Finn pulled the waistband away from his stomach and peered down at Fragar's handle tucked securely away.

"Yes, please!" the two girls cried, while all the guys shouted for him to keep it in his pants.

"Dude, you can't whip that thing out here!" the guy in the chair pleaded, his eyes wide with fear. "This is a national park. They'll arrest you for doing that kind of shit."

"Unfortunately, Tom's right. This is a weapons-free zone *if* you know what I mean." The girl on the towel pouted as she pointed at a small blue sign posted at the closest beach entrance.

It had a picture of a gun with a slashed circle over it. At the bottom of the sign, it read, Weapons-free Zone.

Finn deflated and let the band of his trunks snap closed. "Well, shit. I was hoping to keep it a secret, but if you guys could spot it all the way over there…"

He shrugged. "Nothing more satisfying than that look a guy gets when I whip Fragar out at the last second and extend it right in his face."

Finn chuckled as he remembered one particular thug that had actually shat himself, then run in the opposite direction, holding his pants up with both hands.

"Fragar?" Tom asked, confused.

At the same time, the girl next to him looked sad. "Guy?"

Finn saw his mistake right away. In the dwarven language, there were no male or female pronouns. All dwarves were equal in dwarven eyes. He remembered a talk with Mila where she tried to explain sexism to him. He was pretty sure he understood, but it was a lifetime of habit to break.

"Sorry, miss. I didn't mean to be non-inclusive. Guy *or* girl, it doesn't matter; you come at me, you're going to get Fragar stuck in you one way or another." He winked at her to let her know he was grateful for her correction.

"And we're back in the game, girls!" Margarita Girl said triumphantly.

"What the fuck is a Fragar?" Tom looked a little insane, as if he were not dealing well with the conversation so far.

"Oh, sorry. That's the axe's name. Fragar." He chuckled at the confused faces looking back up at him. "Don't look at me. I didn't name it. You'll have to blame my great-great-uncle Fafnir; he's the one who gave it that moniker."

Tom's eyes went wide. "The fuck?"

"I really wish I could show it to you. It just has the most perfect lines, powerful and graceful at the same time. It's one of the only weapons I've ever seen that can strike fear and admiration at the same time."

"I knew a guy in high school that had one of those," the girl in the chair said, shivering at the memory.

Tom snapped his head her way. *"The fuck?"*

"Fun fact," Finn continued, lost in his people's history. "Fafnir was eventually killed with his own sword, Gram. Man, that is a beautiful sword—three feet of magically imbued gold. Perfect amount of heft to it. Enough that you know it's in your hand, but not so much that you get tired using it, even after hours of swinging it on the battlefield."

"Three feet?" Tom pulled at his hair. "What the fuck are you talking about? It was just a joke, man! I was just fucking with you!"

"No. My bad for not hiding it well enough." Finn waved off Tom's attempt at downplaying the situation. He glanced around the beach, saw that there weren't any other people close by, and decided to take a chance. These nice people deserved a little something for taking the time to talk to him.

Finn leaned in and spoke in a loud whisper. "Look, I know it's against the rules, but you guys have been great, and I feel like it would be a crime not to show you Fragar in all its glory. I figure we're secluded enough that I'm willing to take the chance." He looked at each of them in turn. "What do you say? You guys want to see it?"

There was a general nodding from everyone but Tom, who just sat there, his mouth open and a glazed look to his eyes.

Finn glanced around one more time then reached into his trunks, pulled out Fragar, and whispered the power word. In the blink of an eye, the handle extended, then unfolded several times before snapping into its complete form, glowing with magical purple light as the thousands of runes etched themselves into the blade and haft.

Finn spun the handle to twirl the wide blade of the bearded axe and make the sunlight dance off its polished surface.

As he squatted before the kids, Finn held up the magical axe for all to see. Once he was sure they had all gotten a good look, he whispered the power word again, and Fragar instantly folded back down into its handle.

Finn stood and stuffed the folded axe back into place in his trunks, then smiled down at their slack-jawed faces. "I felt the same way the first time I saw it too! Man, you guys were great, but I have to go. Hope you all have a good one."

He waved and walked on down the beach.

The group sat in silence as they watched the giant man who carried a magical axe in his Speedo walk farther up the beach until he disappeared in the heat shimmers coming off the sand.

A guy in the back, under one of the umbrellas, cleared his throat. "Everyone thought he was talking about his dick, right? That wasn't just me?"

They all nodded and took long drinks of whatever they had on hand.

CHAPTER FIFTEEN

Mila stepped out of Lee's Leather and tugged at the bottom hem of her new moto jacket, admiring the soft, supple texture. She liked the offset zipper that ran up at an angle from her left hip to her left shoulder, leaving the front of the jacket as a single smooth panel of black leather.

The leather pants, on the other hand, would take some getting used to. Although after popping a quick squat to check her movement range, she'd been surprised at how much the soft black hide stretched. To tell the truth, the pants didn't restrict her at all.

Remmy stepped out beside her and Mila had to smile. She had never seen anyone in that much leather who wasn't working at a fetish club. Not that she had ever been to a fetish club, but it was the first example that came to mind.

The goblin had gone with a hooded leather catsuit that had a series of stylish silver buckles up the front to keep it closed, and flared bottoms to fit over the new pair of boots.

Her daggers were hidden under a thin leather duster that was light enough that it flapped in the light breeze. Every bit of leather was dyed black except the dark brown belt and dagger sheaths. She looked like some comic book hero, and Mila thought it was adorable. She had to admit Remmy looked quite attractive in a goth-meets-cowboy kind of way. The whole ensemble was completely over the top and fit Remmy to a tee.

Mila had gone a little more subtle. She'd bought the black moto jacket that covered her corset holster, a white t-shirt, fitted black leather pants, and a pair of boots that felt like she had been wearing them for years, they were so well made.

They'd arrived at the store and a woman had met them at the door, then led them both directly to a changing room where the clothes were already waiting. They'd changed, thrown away their old outfits, and paid with a wad of cash that Mila felt was a little small considering the quality of the garments.

"Okay." Mila headed down the street towards a cafe they had passed on their way to the shop. "Two questions. Why did we go to a custom leather shop for clothes, and how the fuck did they know we were coming and what our sizes are? Actually, there's a third question. Those clothes fit you like a glove. There is no way they had goblin-sized clothes on the rack. What just happened there?"

Remmy laughed. "I told you I had a cousin that worked there, right?"

Mila nodded.

"Well, I texted him and told him what we needed and

that we would be there shortly. He got it all together, and that's that." She started skipping down the hill to keep pace with Mila. "The reason we went to a leather shop is that I knew they would have stuff in my size. If we went to a regular store, then I would have to find stuff that didn't really fit me in the kids' section. I hate clothes that don't fit."

At the café, Mila opened the door for the energetic Remmy. "After you, my lady."

Remmy bowed and flourished her duster behind her with one hand. "Thank you, my lady."

Mila laughed as they stepped inside.

Cafe Rouge was a coffee and sandwich place that seemed to specialize in the French style. Framed posters of the Eiffel Tower and the French countryside adorned several walls, along with a lot of brick and timber construction that was reminiscent of an old-world farmhouse.

They found a table close to the windows along the front of the establishment and sat down. Mila unzipped her jacket but refrained from taking it off, which was one of the biggest drawbacks of carrying concealed weapons.

"Okay, I understand that they had clothes in your proportions, but my question is, why?"

"Oh, because any good leather shop employs goblins as artisans," Remmy explained as if it were obvious.

"What? Why?" Mila hadn't known about that.

"Most leather shops are owned by magicals, and everyone knows the best leatherworkers are goblins. My people have been shaping leather for as long as there has been leather. It's the one art form my people excel at. Plus, if we went to a leather shop, then we could get enchanted gear."

Mila held up the front flap of her moto jacket and looked at it closely. "This is enchanted? To do what?"

"Just simple stuff, like the ability to stretch and heal itself over time."

"It's enchanted to stretch?" Mila was shocked that she had never thought of that being a thing. "They can do that?"

Remmy laughed at her wonder. "Of course they can. Why else would you be able to move so well in those pants?"

"I don't know. I just thought they were really thin or something."

"I like how I said they can stretch *and* heal themselves over time, and it was the stretching part that blew your mind."

Mila chuckled along with her. "Yeah, I suppose that was the odd one to latch onto. I guess living with Danica makes healing magic feel second nature to me. A piece of clothing that heals just seems like the natural thing to do if you're enchanting clothes."

"Oh." Remmy lofted her brows as she remembered something. "I also asked him to make it hydroprofik."

Mila raised an eyebrow. "You mean, 'hydrophobic?'"

"Yeah, that one. Where liquid stuff just falls off and stuff."

"What made you think to ask for that?"

"Well, mostly, it was the impromptu bath we had to take in the alley. Won't have to do that if the blood just rolls off you in the first place."

Mila gave her an approving nod. "Look at the big brain thinking about this one."

Remmy blushed and shrugged. "Just made sense, ya know? You want some food?"

"Sure, just get me a coffee and a sandwich; dealer's choice, I'm not picky. Can I use your phone while you're up there? I need to call in some reinforcements."

Unzipping a pocket on her thigh, Remmy pulled out her phone and handed it over. "You're not one of those people that says they're not picky then don't like what others get for them, are you?"

Mila took the phone and laughed. "No, I'm not, but I know the people you're talking about. Seriously, I'll be happy with whatever you get."

"Cool. Be back in a few."

Mila opened the phone and dialed a number she had memorized for just such an occasion as this. She put the phone to her ear and listened as it rang three times.

"Hello?" a cautious male voice asked.

"Carl? It's Mila."

"Dr. Winters," Carl said, his tone much more friendly. "How are you?"

"Well, that's a complicated question," she admitted.

Carl's deep rolling laugh made Mila smile. "It wouldn't be the real you if it wasn't complicated. What can I do for you?"

"How would you and your team feel about coming out to San Francisco and helping me clear out a few dozen Rougarou, another crazy mage, and save one of my sisters? Again." Mila laughed nervously. "Oh, and there are a few hundred thralls this time."

"Leveling up, are we?" She could hear him scratching his stubble while he thought. "Well, I have to wonder if you have the luck of a rabbit's foot factory. My team was just told to stand down from our deployment; evidently, it was handled on site by the locals. We're on our way to the locker rooms as we speak, still geared up. Give me a second to ask the others."

"Sure." Mila felt tightness in her chest as the anticipation of their answer hung in the air. She hadn't realized how much she was depending on Carl and his people to be free and ready to go. She had just figured it would all work out. Turned out that a lot of very unexpected things had to happen for her wish to be fulfilled, and lo and behold it couldn't have been timed better. That kind of freaked Mila out a little.

"You there?"

Mila was jolted from her thoughts. "Yes, I'm here."

"Where do we meet you?"

Relief flooded through her chest. "We're at a place called Cafe Rouge. I'll have to ask what the full address is, so give me a second."

"It's okay, I found it," Carl quickly informed her. "Be there in twenty minutes. I need to clear this with Preston, but I know there won't be a problem on that end. I'm going to have Nick pick up a tactical vehicle for us to use and meet us there. Sit tight. We'll see you in a bit."

'See you in twenty," Mila confirmed, then hung up as Remmy came back to the table, a tray balanced on one hand.

"We have backup?" she asked, placing a coffee and a baguette sandwich with turkey, mayo, and tomatoes on it.

"Yup. Carl and his people." On remembering that Remmy hadn't met Carl and his people, she added, "They're one of Preston's G.A.E.L. teams."

Remmy set down her own coffee and a bowl of onion soup covered in bubbling cheese. "The big guns, huh? I like it."

Mila licked her lips as she looked longingly at the soup.

Remmy sighed and switched the soup for the sandwich. "I knew you were lying."

"Thank you," Mila said sheepishly in her "cute voice".

Remmy laughed. "Finn's right."

Mila raised an eyebrow. "About what?"

"It's basically impossible to stay mad at you."

"It's my superpower."

"Pretty sure magic is yer superpower."

Mila laughed. "That too."

CHAPTER SIXTEEN

As they sat at the large reclaimed wood table off Rebecca and Lance's kitchen, the warm spring breeze blowing through the elevated house, Penny and Rebecca poured over several handwritten books along with stacks of sketches and diagrams on faded yellowing paper.

Lance and Grimmly worked in the kitchen to make sandwiches and a creamy broccoli and cheese soup for lunch. The father and son joked with each other quietly enough not to bother Rebecca and Penny while they worked.

Penny's mouth watered at the smells of soup and deli meats as they reminded her that she had a lot of magic that needed refilling. She hoped that they made extra because Penny would need it before she headed back home.

Rebecca slid one of the books over to Penny and pointed at a page covered in tight script around a sketch of a robed Drude. "This is from one of my first ancestors to take passage on Earth, Gregory Geralt. It's the account of the last fight between this Azoth and the Valkyries. He talks about how the Valkyries were convinced that Azoth was dead, and called the matter closed, but Gregory was convinced that it wasn't that simple. When he brought up his concerns to the sisterhood, they refused to listen to him and told him to drop it."

"Chi? Shir shee. *Why didn't they believe him? He must have had some compelling evidence to go to them with his concern.*" A loud growl from Penny's stomach punctuated the question. She slapped her hands to her belly and grinned in embarrassment.

"I'm so sorry, Penny. I totally forgot that Dragons convert their food to magic. After your flight here, you must be starving. Lance, can you grab a bag of chips for Penny? Oh, and grab me the Oreos."

Penny brightened. "Shir. *Thanks. I didn't want to be rude and ask, but I am feeling the need to refuel.*"

Rebecca laughed and adjusted the wide-neck knit shirt she had put on over her bikini top. The taupe-colored shirt hung off her left shoulder and had become caught on a necklace that Penny hadn't noticed when she arrived. In fact, Penny was sure Rebecca hadn't been wearing it until she had gone to her bedroom to grab the shirt.

Rebecca pulled the necklace out from under her shirt collar, giving Penny a view of the pendant hanging on the thin gold chain. It was a variation of an old Norse symbol called a Gungnir that represented the spear of Odin and looked like a square standing on its corner with an X over it.

Rebecca's version, however, had a thinner diamond shape instead of a square, and the angles of the X were much steeper. In addition, the top two lines of the X came back together to form a second point at the top.

Normally, Penny wouldn't think anything of seeing a variation of a relatively common symbol, but this variation was a symbol Penny knew very well. It still represented the spear Gungnir, but this was the original symbol, as well as the centerpiece of the spear creator's family crest. The crest of the Dwarven Emperor. Finn's family crest.

Penny stored that detail away for later but knew it must have some kind of significance.

Lance set a bowl filled with Nacho Cheese Doritos beside Penny and a plate with a couple of stacks of cream-filled chocolate cookies beside his wife. She gave him a quick kiss before he walked back to the kitchen to stir the soup.

Rebecca scanned the book a few pages ahead. "As far as I can tell, the only reason the Valkyrie didn't believe him was that he was trying to explain how the Drude and Valkyries are very similar, and more than likely have an ancestor in common."

"Squee, shir? *Wait, he thought the Drude and the Valkyries are from the same bloodline?*" Penny stopped herself from stuffing a Dorito in her face just long enough to get the question out.

Rebecca read a few more passages. "Uh, yeah, it looks like he did. Though "bloodline" really isn't the right word. More like they came from the same source. Both Drude and Valkyries are not necessarily a race, so much as an entity that finds a body. Just like Valkyries always inhabit Peabrain bodies, the Drude do the same with whatever race that is. So, if a Valkyrie comes back, why wouldn't a Drude?"

Penny immediately saw the error in the logic. "Chi chi. Shiri. *Yes, but there are Peabrains here on Earth for the returning Valkyries to inhabit, but not so with the Drude. As far as my research shows, he's the only one that's ever been on Earth.*"

"I was thinking that too," Rebecca said around a bite of Oreo, "but Gregory actually addresses that. He argues that the Valkyries and Drude don't actually take a body, but have one created out of their energy. After all, everything in the universe is energy, just in various states of existence. Maybe a Valkyrie *is* the same person from life to life; they're just put together differently each time."

"Chi shee? *Let's say this is true. How did this help Gregory understand how to get rid of the Drude permanently?*"

Rebecca quickly chewed the rest of the cookie, brushed the crumbs from her fingers onto a white linen napkin, then pointed out a particular passage. "He laid it out here. Basically, the main difference between Valkyries and Drude, besides their opposed magic types, is that while Valkyries exist in the physical world completely, Drude only half-exist in a corporeal state. The rest of them is in a place between realities. The way Gregory describes it, this sounds a bit like Purgatory. That part doesn't really matter; what's important is that because of this difference, they manifest powers in different ways."

"*How so?*" Penny raised an eye ridge as she chomped on another chip and felt relieved when the calorie-dense snack broke down into raw magic in her belly to refill her reserves.

"If I'm reading this right, then a good way to describe their main characteristics would be to say that Valkyries are fast, and Drude are powerful. Valkyries come back quickly after death, work best in large numbers, and are able to adapt to situations given the right circumstances, but they lack personal power when it comes to magic. The Drude, on the other hand, take forever to come back, work best as individuals, and are able to conform those around them to their will. Because they are half in this other realm, they can pull power from vast stores they keep hidden away. Really, the only thing holding back a Drude's power is the physical form's ability to channel that power through it. They need to feed their corporeal body raw power to grow strong enough to gain access to their full potential."

Penny frowned, chomping on another chip while she thought about that. "Squee shee shir. *So, how does that info help us? It sounds like no matter what, a part of a Drude will survive to come back.*"

"Well, that's where ol' Gregory had a theory." Rebecca turned the page to reveal a diagram of a hand-held device that looked a bit like a steampunk version of a Thermal Detonator. "He argued that Drude *must* have the ability to become fully corporeal, because they are actually born at some point, and only develop powers when they hit the equivalent of puberty, just like Valkyries do. When in this fully corporeal form, they would be vulnerable because they are completely cut off from their magic. If they have no magic when they die, there is no way they can retreat back into that place between realities. He designed this device to force them to transition completely. He guessed the effect would only last for a few seconds, but he was never able to test that—not only because the Drude was gone by then, but because the device would take celestial magic to power it."

Penny looked up from the plans, a big toothy smile on her face. "Chi chi! *I just happen to know a girl...*"

Rebecca laughed. "That's kind of the point of you being here, I suppose."

"Let's clear the table." Lance came over with his hands full of bowls of soup and plates of sandwiches. "We can all get to work on building this thing after lunch when Grimm heads in for his nap."

"I don't want to take a nap!" Grimmly climbed into his chair opposite Penny.

"You will when you have a belly full of carbs, buddy." Lance set Grimmly's plate down and tucked a napkin into his shirt collar. "There you go, bud. Ready to get to work."

Penny smiled at the little boy. He smiled back, then nearly spilled his entire bowl of soup trying to get his spoon through the melted cheese and the crouton underneath. A quick flick of her talon and Penny magically bonded the bowl to the table, making it impossible to tip without tipping the entire table.

"Thanks for that." Rebecca indicated the bowl. "You have no idea how much food has hit this floor."

"*It's no problem.*" A smoke ring rose from a nostril.

"Do you have any kids of your own?" Lance dipped his sandwich in his soup before taking a bite.

Penny grinned. "Chi shee. Shee. *Not yet. Soon though.*"

She absent-mindedly rubbed her stomach with a hand. "*Very soon.*"

CHAPTER SEVENTEEN

Mila finished her soup and took a sip of coffee, then leaned back and crossed her arms. "How do you deal with living in a tribe?"

Remmy looked up from her sandwich and raised an eyebrow. She swallowed her bite and took a drink of water to wash it down. "I don't really deal with it; it's just the way I was raised. Why?"

Mila bit her lip as she stared off into the distance. "I was just thinking about how working with the Valkyries is more irritating that satisfying most of the time. I was just wondering if it gets easier."

"Oh, I guess I can understand that part. Sometimes in the tribe, there's someone that's an elder that really gets on your nerves. It sucks, but it's only temporary."

"What do you mean?" Mila took another sip of coffee. It was an excellent roast. She hoped she could get a bag to take home for Finn; it was strong without being bitter and had a sweet, fruity aftertaste.

"Well, the point of elders is that they got old with expe-

rience and pass that experience down to the next genera-
tion, then they die, and the ones under them become the
elders. If someone annoys you, all you have to do is outlive
them."

Mila barked a bitter laugh. "Then I am well and truly
fucked. Valkyries are basically immortal. Unless we leave
Earth, the sisters I have right now are the sisters I'll have
forever. And to top it all off, it's always going to be either
Victoria or Missy who's in charge, and both of them treat
me like I'm a child. It's so frustrating."

Remmy sniffed, then shrugged. "That sucks, I guess. But
you have to admit, compared to them, you *are* a child."

"No, compared to them, I am young and maybe lack
experience, but I am an accomplished woman in my thirties, with a doctorate in anthropology that got me a leading
position at an internationally renowned museum. I also
stopped the Dark Star, using my Valkyrie powers just days
after learning I even had them. I didn't see the sisterhood
out there tracking that crazy witch down. My point is I'm
capable and can get a lot of shit done if I put my mind to it,
but they treat me like I don't know how to wipe my own
ass." Mila angrily flicked a crumb off the table. "The worst
part is my 'elder sister' looks like some little goth punk,
and it's really hard to take her seriously. If she's so old and
wise, why would she continue to act like that? She must
know it's distracting."

"What's so distracting about her?" Remmy pulled out
her phone. "What's her last name?"

"Walker. Missy Walker. I know she's from SoCal, but
she could tone it down a little. At least stop dying her hair
electric blue and wear a skirt that comes down more than

an inch past her ass cheeks. I know I shouldn't be judging her by the way she dresses, but dude, she's the leader of an ancient sisterhood of Valkyries; at least act like it."

"Weren't you a goth in high school?" Remmy typed on her phone.

Mila flushed pink. "Yeah, but that just proves my point. I stopped dressing that way as soon as I started college. I needed people to take me seriously if I was going to excel in my chosen field."

"Well, the question is, if you didn't have to impress strangers to get ahead, would you still be dressing like that?"

Mila frowned and bit the inside of her lip while she thought about it. "I mean, I did look pretty cute."

"That sounds like a yes to me."

"Fine, I suppose I would still wear the occasional black lipstick if I thought I could get away with it. What's your point?"

Remmy looked up from her phone and locked eyes with Mila. The look made Mila sit up a little straighter and take notice. There was a motherly quality to the goblin's gaze that Mila hadn't seen before.

"My point is, if there is one woman that doesn't have to worry about what people think, it would be the eldest sister of a group of women who've been alive longer than the Earth has existed. It sounds like you're jealous."

Mila's mouth dropped open in shock. She stared at Remmy, who just looked back down at her phone and continued to scroll through a web page as if she had not just verbally smacked the shit out of Mila.

As she took a long, deep look inward, Mila asked

herself whether Remmy was right or wrong. She wanted to dismiss Remmy's words as ridiculous, but to her dismay, Mila thought the little goblin might be right.

With a wash of revelation, Mila realized that she still held a big wad of resentment that she'd had to change her identity just to be taken seriously.

She remembered that first week at college; a painful series of interactions with dismissive teachers and administrators that left her feeling ashamed of trying to express herself.

Putting her clothes and makeup in a box in the back of her closet had been like betraying a best friend who had stuck with her through all the difficult times of her adolescence. She had conformed to strangers' expectations out of fear that they would reject her, and all it cost was her sense of adventure.

Decisions throughout her life influenced by that heart-wrenching act began to pop into her head. Her choice to wear muted colors so she wouldn't stand out. Never buying the fun version of things when a perfectly boring version was available just so people wouldn't think she was weird. Hell, until Danica had taken her to the mall and forced her to buy some "sexy" underwear, she had only bought the most boring kinds she could get her hands on because that was what people expected of a Doctor of Anthropology.

She had completely stopped using clothing to express herself out of fear.

Mila's brows lowered in anger. Fuck those judgmental pricks. They had stolen something from her because they didn't want to feel uncomfortable talking to a girl who had the audacity to dress the way she wanted. They had taken advantage of a young woman who was just trying to figure out who she was.

Not anymore. She was the master of her own destiny.

A smile crept onto her lips. She was going to take Danica shopping as soon as she got home.

"You're right," Mila said, crossing her arms. "It was my issue. Missy can dress however she wants."

"So, you're all good with her now?" Remmy looked up with a smile.

"Oh, no. She's still insufferable, but I now know that blaming the way she dresses has nothing to do with how I feel about her. That's another issue altogether." Mila narrowed her eyes. "How did you know I needed to hear that?"

"I went through the same thing back in my thirties. Conformed to a "higher standard" so I would be taken seriously. It took me nearly fifteen more years to understand that I was taken seriously because I was the best at what I did. No one in my tribe can hold a candle to my moves." She laughed. "Can you believe I was too scared to get naked in front of others until I was forty?"

"I'm going to be honest. I can't imagine a shy Remmy. Like, at all. I'm pretty sure I've seen your ass more than my own over the last year."

Remmy laughed and shook her shoulders at Mila in a suggestive way. "You gotta be proud of what you've got, and if you're not, you have to figure out how to love yourself enough to get there."

"Damn, Remmy. When did you get so wise?"

She shrugged. "You learn a lot in forty-eight years. Sometimes listening to your elders is a good thing."

Mila laughed. "I always forget you're older than me."

"It's my youthful complexion."

"Yeah. It is." Mila laughed.

The bell over the door rang, and Carl and his team walked in, scanning the cafe for Mila.

Mila waved her arm over her head to get the group's attention. They picked their way between the tables with care not to knock into anyone with the large black duffel bags each of them carried.

Mila stood to meet them and gave each a quick hug. She then pointed out Remmy to the group. "Guys, this is my good friend, Remmy. Remmy, this is Carl, Tina, Howard, and Jenny. I assume Nick is on his way?"

"He said he would be here in about five minutes." Carl checked his watch.

"You guys want a coffee or something?" Mila waved a hand at her half-empty cup on the table. "It's really good."

"I could go for one," Howard admitted as he licked his lips.

"Me too," Tina added.

Carl pulled out a fifty from his wallet and handed it to Tina. "Why don't you get to-go cups for all of us. I'm sure Nick will want one too."

Carl and Jenny took a seat as the other two went up to the counter to place the order. He stowed his bag under his chair and leaned in as Jenny pulled out a tablet and powered it on.

"Okay, what's the sitrep?" Carl asked.

Mila gave a quick recap of what had happened since her

nightmare that morning and ended with them escaping the factory.

"What's the address of the factory?" Jenny asked, tablet at the ready.

Remmy pulled out her phone and opened the map app, found the building quickly, and showed it to the elf woman. Jenny entered the info. A few seconds later, she laid the tablet down on the table so they could all see it.

Mila was surprised when a set of blueprints for the factory loaded. "How the hell do you have blueprints for this place?"

"Most buildings' blueprints are out there for the taking. You just have to know where to look and how to get in when you find them." Jenny nodded with a wink to make her pink ponytail bounce.

"Can you point out where the targets were gathered?" Carl was all business.

Jenny sobered up and made notes on the screen as Mila told them what she could.

"The place was pretty big, though, so they might have more in another section of the building."

Carl considered then shook his head. "Doubtful. While it is a large building, it's relatively small for a factory. Most of the space is just this one large area, with a few administration areas, like where you ran into the thralls. The whole building is roughly fifty by a hundred meters, not a lot of room to withdraw if things go badly. You said there were old machines blocking off parts of the building?"

"Well, I don't know that they were set up to block anything. I think they were just left to rot where they had been installed along the walls. We could use them for cover, though; those things were solid steel. The center area was open, though."

"We have to be careful of the wards," Remmy said out of the blue.

Mila blinked in surprise. "What wards?"

"You didn't see em? They were all over the outside. Most of them were disguised as graffiti, but I saw a couple that would make teleporting in impossible."

Carl sighed. "You do like the hard missions, don't you, Mila?"

She smiled. "I wouldn't need your help if they were easy."

"Fair point."

"Hey, Nick's here." Tina informed them as she came over to the table with a drink carrier full of white paper coffee cups.

"Okay, we can assess the situation better onsite. You ready?"

Mila nodded, then leaned over to Remmy. "Hey, can I borrow some money?"

Remmy didn't even ask her what it was for, just nodded and handed over the much-diminished roll of cash.

Two minutes later, Mila came out of the cafe and jogged across the street to the waiting white sprinter van, a pound of the delicious coffee beans in her hand. She decided Finn deserved a treat after all the work he was putting in for Penny.

"Hi, Nick. Okay, let's go." She climbed into the back of the van with the rest of them.

CHAPTER EIGHTEEN

Mila watched through the van's windshield as Howard casually strolled past the factory and glanced at the large brick structure. When he had passed the building, he crossed the street. His long orc legs ate up the distance quickly as he headed down a side street in order to circle back to the van.

Remmy had been right about the graffiti. The entire bottom ten feet of the faded white bricks had been covered in some extremely impressive street art. After watching Penny create several wards for the condo, Mila could now pick out several similar sigils painted between the more elaborate murals.

While they waited for Howard to return, the team changed from their street clothes into their black tactical gear, strapping wands and guns where they needed to. The number of flying elbows and knees as four people changed clothes in the back of a van prompted Mila and Remmy to move into the front seat. As she looked over her shoulder from the passenger seat into the back, Mila could see that the team was nearly dressed and kitted out.

Something about the view made her eyes water. She blinked a few times as she tried to determine what was so odd about the angle.

"Is the back of this van larger on the inside than it should be?"

Where the cabin connected to the storage space, filled with racks of equipment and a small desk built into the walls, the view seemed warped, almost like looking at an object through a glass of water. The whole image was there, but the proportions didn't make sense to her brain.

"Yeah." Tina strapped her pistol to her thigh. "We use these things for long-term surveillance. Having five people crammed into a regular van for days on end wouldn't work out for anyone. We can crank up the effect and add a second room with cots and a toilet, but it amplifies the distortion effect and makes using the side doors impossible. If you're not used to it, the effect can make you pretty sick."

"That's so cool!" Remmy's grin nearly touched her ears.

"Pretty useful, but dangerous if done improperly."

The side door slid open and the huge form of Howard jumped in and closed the door behind him. He had already changed into his black pants and shirt before he had left, but he pulled off the brown Carhartt and began strapping his utility harness over his shoulders while he reported what he found.

"It's a powerful set of wards. Blocks all teleporting in or out of the building unless authorized. Additionally, there's a ward that will set off a pretty nasty series of traps if we try and enter the building, although that one looks like it's one way."

"We didn't set anything off when we ran out of the second-floor side door," Mila confirmed.

Howard nodded, strapping his pistol to his thigh. "On top of all that, there are alarms attached to all the wards that will instantly alert whoever's in the building."

"Any good news?" Carl asked, his face sour.

"Actually, yeah. It's a powerful series of wards, but in its power, there's a flaw. Each ward supports the ones around it. It's like a scaffold; each part supports the others to create a strong structure, but at the same time, if you remove one piece, the whole thing comes tumbling down."

Mila snorted a laugh. "So, all we have to do is set it off, and then we don't have to worry about setting it off?"

"Pretty much." Howard chuckled.

Mila bit her lip and looked out the passenger side window trying to think of a way inside. They had parked close to the mouth of an alley between two rows of businesses with apartments on top. The whole city was set up that way for the most part. San Francisco had run out of land years ago, so they had built up instead of out. Everywhere you looked, as much housing and commerce had been crammed into every nook and cranny as they feasibly could. That meant that there was a lot of trash for a given area.

As she stared into the alley, Mila saw that there were several dumpsters full to the top with garbage bags from the apartments above and loose scraps of food from the restaurant on the ground floor. In the warm spring air, all that garbage was a perfect breeding ground for flies. A black cloud of the things swarmed in and out of the dumpster as they searched for food and places to lay their eggs.

Mila's eyebrow rose as the beginnings of a plan formed in her mind.

"How big would something have to be to set off the wards?" Mila looked at Howard. "I assume they don't want them going off every time a rat strolls in."

"True," the orc said, scratching at his chin as he did the math in his head. Even with a concealment spell, Howard's Orcish features were slightly too large, so it took a second to fully stroke his large chin. "If I had to guess, I would say anything bigger than a cat would be enough."

"Perfect!" Nick threw his hands up in victory. "I'll just shift into my weasel form and slip in to take a quick look."

Howard shook his head in the negative. "Wouldn't work. You'd set those things off no matter how small you make yourself. There's a ward specifically to look for magical potential in the creatures. You might be the size of a weasel, but your aura would give you away in a second."

"What about a whole bunch of little lifeforms all at once?" Mila lofted one brow.

"That would work, but they would have to be packed together pretty tightly."

"We still need to get a lay of the land inside there," Carl interjected. "Would I be able to send a bubble drone in?"

Howard shook his head.

Carl frowned. "Figures."

"I think I have something, but I don't know how well it'll work," Mila said with a half-smile. "I can ask one of those flies to go take a look for us."

She pointed at the fly-encrusted dumpster.

Carl's eyes narrowed. "You can do that?"

"I can, but I don't know how well it will be able to report what it sees. My magic seems to enhance an insect's intelligence while I talk to it, but it only goes so far. Plus, it's a fly, not exactly the brightest of insects. They're basically instinct machines."

Carl looked to the rest of the group. "Can anyone think of a reason not to try it?"

Everyone shook their heads in the negative.

"Go for it." Carl took a seat on the small swivel chair at the desk. "How long do you think it will take?"

"I have no idea."

Mila turned back around, settled into her seat, and focused on the cloud of flies. Not really knowing how to get one particular fly's attention, especially from a distance, she decided to use a little magic to try and focus down on one individual and bring it over to the van so she could explain what she needed from it. She just needed to get its attention.

Not knowing what she was doing but having a basic idea in her head to try, she gathered a tiny portion of magic in her mind. With the drop of power acting as a communication node, she sent out another, even smaller portion of magic so as not to overwhelm the little insect's primitive mind.

Through the focused drop she held in her mind, she could feel the second wisp of power shoot out away from her, crossing the short distance in a flash to slam into a particularly large specimen.

Mila gasped as she could see and hear what the fly experienced. She opened her eyes and felt a moment of vertigo as she saw two images at once. The double vision wasn't too bad until she turned her head and her brain suddenly couldn't process the two views at the same time. Bile rose to the back of her throat. She quickly closed her eyes so she could deal with only one image.

Her stomach settled, and she focused on the odd experience.

She realized the fly hadn't moved since the connection was made, and she wondered if she had somehow broken its mind. She thought about how freaky it would be to see herself through the fly's eyes. She let out a squeak as the fly spun around to face the van.

"Are you okay?" Remmy put her hand on Mila's arm.

Mila nodded and smiled. "This is so freaky. I think I just possessed a fly. Hang on, let me try something."

She sent her will through the connection and made the fly shoot forward, then turn in a circle, followed by a barrel roll.

She laughed with giddy excitement. "This is crazy! I have complete control of this thing. I'm going to take it inside and scope things out."

"Wait," Howard warned. "How much magic did you put into that fly?"

"Barely any at all. Not even enough to make a spark."

"First, that's fucking impressive," the orc said in his deep monotone. "Second, you're probably good to pass through the wards."

"Probably?"

"Ninety-nine percent. More actually," he amended. "Every animal has at least a small bit of magic in them, so the wards would account for that."

"Okay. I'm off."

Mila willed the insect to fly across the road, then began scouting the outside of the building, looking for anything they might have missed.

The warped vision of the fly's prismatic eyes was not nearly as hard to comprehend as Mila had thought. She guessed most of the vision processing was being done by the fly, and she was getting more of an integrated view than the actual view. It was the only thing that made sense to her. She had seen demonstrations of what flies see at the museum. Looking through the little prismatic spyglass at the display had given her an instant headache, but this wasn't so bad.

A lap around the building went far quicker than she thought possible, but the little fly could really move when she gave it a direction. Flies were quick, but Mila realized that this one was not doing its normal haphazard ducks and dodges that flies did to keep themselves from being too predictable and have a bird snatch them out of the air. Mila gave the haphazard flight pattern a shot, just for realism, and almost puked. It looked like she would just have to be a predictable fly.

After checking the ground level, she shot up to the roof to see if there were any nasty tricks up there, but it looked clear.

Not having any more reasons to stall, she found a broken window among the panes of glass that wrapped all the way around the top of the building. With a deep breath and the hope that she wasn't going to set off the wards, she shot through the opening and into the relative darkness of the factory.

From close to the ceiling, the wide angle of the fly's perspective made the interior look huge.

"Hand me a tablet and a pen." Mila held out a hand but kept her eyes closed. "Actually, pull up the blueprints. I'll mark everything on there."

A tablet and stylus were placed in her hand. She put them in her lap while she flew to one corner of the building and looked down so she could memorize a small section of the machinery layout. She opened her eyes and began to mark everything on the image of the blueprints.

Mila quickly realized that she didn't have to memorize the layout, just use her double vision to focus from one to the other, and fill out each part of the layout.

She found the Rougarou pack in the center of the building. They were quiet, most of them taking naps in big piles of black fur and talons. She did a quick count and marked that spot on the blueprint with a sixty-seven.

The storeroom where they had run into the thralls had been cleared of its shelves. Those huge metal monstrosities had been pushed flat against the walls. The more than three hundred thralls now stood in a large, tight-packed circle in the middle of the room.

Mila marked it all down, including the several doors that had been welded shut either by the previous tenants or Azoth's people.

She realized she was stalling again, not wanting to see how bad off Victoria was.

Mila steeled herself and flew over to the last section of the factory to take an accounting.

CHAPTER NINETEEN

Mila's fly closed in on two figures in a cleared-out section of the factory floor. She directed the fly to get close enough that she could hear, but not so close that it would be noticed. She ended up about ten feet above and behind Yaminah's left shoulder as she faced the bound Valkyrie.

Mila cringed at the sight of Victoria, still hanging from her shackles, covered in sweat and grime from the dusty building. Her hair was stringy and stuck to her face. But it was her hands that made Mila nearly burst into tears.

In the hour since Mila had seen her last, her hands had swollen to twice their normal size and split open in several places from the internal pressure. Blood dripped from her fingers down into her hair and onto the floor below. It had to be excruciating.

Victoria had a permanent twist of pain on her face but didn't cry out. She didn't even raise her voice but talked to Yaminah in a calm and steady voice.

"You don't have to do this," Victoria said, tone matter of

fact. "We have a way to fix what he has done to your soul. We can repair the damage and free—"

"Do you know how it works when a Drude takes a thrall?" Yaminah interrupted. "I found it fascinating, considering I didn't even know what a Drude was a few weeks ago. But my education has been rather hands-on since then."

As she paced, Yaminah held up a single finger. "The first way they can take someone is to make them into a simple thrall. It works on anyone, magical or not. He just takes all but a sliver of their essence and replaces what he took with infernal magic. Boom, instant minion. Low maintenance, never question orders."

She held up a second finger. "Two. A Drude can take the whole soul and replace it with infernal magic. This may sound like just a different kind of mindless thrall, but I was surprised to find that it's an entirely different process. You see, once he takes the whole soul out, he can then reshape the body into something else entirely. Azoth favors Rougarou, and I can see the appeal. They're strong and deadly, but your people already know all about that. What you might *not* know is that Rougarou are really high maintenance. Need to feed them all the time, and if you're not careful, they can get away from you."

She stopped pacing and turned to look Victoria in the eye, then held up three fingers. "And last but not least, there's what he has done to me. Takes just a bit of the soul and replaces it with infernal magic. The benefits of this to him are very high, but also it costs a fortune in magical resources. I'm still mostly who I was before he took that little part and replaced it with his taint, but he has to use a lot of his magical resources to keep me in line. To be honest, I could probably break free of his control if I really tried. At least I could break the mental control, but there is one tiny hitch. It's so simple, yet so effective. Part of the deal is a Geas. It's a pretty simple spell, at least it is for Azoth. Basically, it's a curse. If I don't do my best to protect him or try to disobey a direct order, the Geas kills me on the spot."

She held up a finger, stopping Victoria from speaking. "Before you say anything more, I feel I should mention that his last order was: in the event that you try to escape or talk your way out of your predicament, I am to hurt you until you stop. Do you understand what I'm saying?"

Victoria nodded, but her face was still passive. "I understand. You understand that you don't have to keep living this way, right? If you take the shackles off, I can have you back to your old self in minutes."

Yaminah sighed loudly, pinching the bridge of her nose. "I just told you what was going to happen if you continued to try to get free."

"You can fight him," Victoria urged, her tone soothing as if she were talking to a wild animal. "We can fight him together. You would be free."

Quick as a cat, Yaminah lunged forward and slammed a fist into Victoria's gut, driving the wind from her lungs.

Mouth open in pain as she swung back on the long chain like a pendulum, Victoria struggled to suck in a breath.

Yaminah caught Victoria by the front of her blouse when she swung back and pulled her in close. "Are you done?"

Victoria finally sucked in a deep breath. "Just set me free, and I'll do the same for you."

Yaminah sighed again and slowly squatted down, keeping eye contact with Victoria. She reached out and pulled off one of Victoria's black heels, tossing the shoe into a dark corner of the factory. Still holding eye contact, Yaminah gave her a sad smile and gently began stroking the top of Victoria's foot.

"I know what you're trying to do, Valkyrie. You want me to get out of control and kill you by accident. It was a good plan, really." She stopped stroking Victoria's foot and took hold of her long slender second toe. "The problem with that plan is that I know exactly how much of a body I can destroy and keep the person alive. It's amazing what you learn growing up in a war zone."

Yaminah twisted her hand savagely to the side, snapping the delicate phalanges, and finally elicited a scream of pain from the ancient Valkyrie.

Mila had seen enough; they needed to get in there now.

Pulling her control from the fly, Mila felt a wave of dizziness overcome her for a second. She caught herself before she fell out of the van's passenger seat, but just barely.

"What happened?" Remmy asked, helping Mila to sit up straight again. "You were filling out the blueprint, then just went silent."

Mila noticed the tablet was gone but spotted it in Carl's hand as he and Tina studied the interior elements Mila had filled in, to come up with a plan of attack.

"We need to get in there now! Victoria is trying to get

Yaminah to kill her, but it's not going to work. She's just being tortured for no reason but her own stubbornness."

"Hey," Jenny said, putting a gentle hand on Mila's shoulder as she leaned into the van's cabin. "Think of this from Victoria's perspective. As far as she knows she's all alone, waiting for some maniac to come back and eat her soul. She doesn't know there's a rescue team right outside. To her, this is her only option."

Mila nodded and wiped a tear from her eye. "I know. You're right. It's just hard to wait while we put our plan together, knowing she's in there suffering because I didn't move fast enough."

"That's not helpful thinking," Jenny admonished. "Think constructively. What can you do while you wait to speed things up later? I'm preparing explosive traps. I'm not entirely sure what we're going to need, but I can get most of the work done while I wait and only have to make little adjustments once we're out there."

Mila glanced at the alley. "I hear you. Thanks."

She patted Jenny's hand and smiled up at her. "Hey, Carl. Just so you know, I can use a shit ton of flies to set off the wards, if that helps with the plan."

His eyes widened, and he nodded. "That would be perfect, actually."

"Okay, let me know when you have a plan of attack ready. I'm going to be gathering our distraction."

Mila gave Carl a nod and turned back to the front seat. Remmy had her nose buried in her phone, a frown on her face.

"What's wrong?"

Remmy looked up from her phone. "Oh, nothing, I guess."

"What are you doing?"

"I was looking for Missy on some of the social media sites, but I can't find anything."

Mila raised an eyebrow. "Why?"

"I just wanted to see what she looked like." The goblin frowned. "It's really weird that I can't find her anywhere. There are Missy Walkers, but none who match the description and age. It's so weird."

"It's not that weird. Maybe she just doesn't have an online presence. She is, like, ten thousand years old. She's probably just over it."

Remmy frowned. "But you said that Valkyries don't regain their memories until they're pretty much grown up."

"Yeah."

"So, up until a few months ago for all Missy knew, she was a regular fifteen-year-old. You're telling me that a fifteen-year-old goth chick from Southern California doesn't have social media? That might actually be the craziest thing I've ever heard from you, boss."

Mila shrugged. "I don't know what to tell you. Look, we can search for her together later if it's bothering this much. Right now, I need to gather a swarm."

Mila sucked in a breath and focused on the flies, formulating just how she was going to take over a million flies all at once.

She cracked her neck and got started.

CHAPTER TWENTY

Finn had been walking up the beach for more than an hour. He had passed from the park into the National Seashore a few miles back. The beachgoers had quickly thinned to nothing, and he hadn't seen a soul for forty-five minutes.

To his left, he could see a short ten-foot-high bluff about five hundred yards inland that was covered in low sturdy trees.

He pulled the pack off his back, set it on the ground, and dug in the main compartment to find his phone. He pulled up the file Penny had sent him and read through some of her notes, then looked over the map she had included in the file.

The bluffs were mentioned in several treasure trails she had highlighted. He double-checked the map to his location and decided he was in the right place.

As he put the phone in his pack, Finn closed his eyes and focused his power, trying to sense high concentrations of precious metals in the area. To his surprise, there were several sources relatively close by. By far, the strongest came from the bluffs. He just needed to find a—

"You okay there, big fella?" a sweet feminine voice asked.

Finn's eyes snapped open as he turned to see a thin young woman in a park ranger outfit. Her sharp features had weathered some from constantly being outside. Her skin was a deep bronze color that matched her sun-streaked brown hair almost perfectly. She stood a few feet away, a cautious look in her brown eyes.

"Oh, hello. Yes, I'm doing quite well. How are you this fine afternoon, Ranger?" Finn gave her his most winning smile.

She raised an amused eyebrow. "I'm doing pretty well. Just a warning, if you're going to continue that way, it's another fifteen miles before you'll reach anything resembling civilization. I don't recommend it, personally."

"Thanks. I don't plan on heading all the way up. I was just out for a long stroll. What about you?" He looked around at the empty beach.

"I'm out surveying the ponies. Getting a rough count and seeing that they don't need medical attention."

Finn nodded. "Well, don't let me keep you. I'm just out for a stroll."

Her eyes narrowed as she regarded him.

"Yeah, you mentioned that." She stared at him for a few seconds more, but he just smiled at her. "Well, if you get into any trouble, I'll be back this way in an hour or so."

"Good to know. Thanks."

She nodded, her expression still suspicious, but turned and headed towards a dune farther inland where a four-wheeler was parked on the back side. He watched as she climbed on, started it up, and after giving him a wave, drove back the way she had just come.

Finn watched her go until he couldn't see her anymore, then turned back towards the bluffs, to look for the best way to get there. He saw where a wash had cut a path through the marsh and spilled out onto the beach.

The waterway was as dry as a bone and would make for easy going, at least part of the way.

He picked up his backpack and shouldered it. After adjusting his floppy hat, he headed inland towards the dried-out wash.

Where the sand turned rough, full of sticks and dried grasses, Finn pulled the leather flip- flops out and tossed them on the ground. He fished his toes under the straps one at a time before continuing onto more solid ground.

On cresting a small dune, Finn saw the marsh spread out between him and the bluffs, the long green grasses waving in the breeze. A strong smell of salt and fresh earth filled his nostrils. He could see the wash wound along the side of the marsh, hemmed in by shoulder-high grass, but it turned back towards the edge of the bluffs where it most likely originated.

He shrugged the pack higher on his shoulders and headed down into the sandy wash, glad to find that it was indeed solid ground compared to the soft give of the beach. Twenty feet into the marsh, he felt like he was walking down a wide hallway with dense grass for the walls.

The grass passage blocked off the sounds of the ocean, only to replace them with the constant slither of grass rubbing against itself in the breeze and the buzz of tiny insects that flourished in the wetlands.

Finn quickly learned to keep his mouth closed as he walked around a sharp bend in the dried creek bed, watching his feet so he didn't trip on a rock, and ran face-first into a dense swarm of gnats. So shocked by the sudden cloud of bugs was he that he sucked in a breath of surprise. That proved to be a huge mistake. It took him nearly five minutes of coughing and spitting to clear his throat and lungs of the tiny intruders.

After that, Finn was much more careful about his mouth etiquette as he traversed the marsh.

As he rounded what he hoped was the final bend before he could get out of the never-ending grass hallway, Finn came to an abrupt halt.

In a tight circle, their heads close together as if they had just been talking quietly to one another, stood five round-bellied ponies.

The ponies and Finn stared at one another with wide eyes as if they had been caught with their hands in the cookie jar. No one moved, unsure what to do next.

Finn finally broke the spell by smiling and giving them a wave. "Hello, everyone. Sorry, didn't mean to interrupt; just passing through."

He slowly walked to the far side of the wash and held his hands up to show he didn't mean them any harm. The five potbellied ponies followed him with their eyes but made no move to get away. Finn sidestepped past them, their judgmental eyes on his every movement.

Once past them, he waved again. "It was a real pleasure,

guys. Please, continue with whatever it was you were doing before I interrupted."

The closest pony whinnied, shook his long mane at Finn, and then headed down the wash in the opposite direction. Finn had the distinct impression that he had a look of disgust on his face.

When the rest of the ponies followed the first one's lead and turned their noses up at him before trotting off like a pack of aristocrats, Finn frowned and gave them all the finger behind their backs.

"Pompous little fucks." He turned back to the path and kicked his foot out to let a pebble fall out of the flip-flop before moving on.

Eventually the wash led to a large lagoon full of lapping ocean water, cut off from the bay itself by the constantly shifting sands of the island. Finn guessed the lagoon didn't have a name, considering how often the landscape must change.

The only way to have any sort of permanent land feature on a sandy barrier island like Assateague must be if a cluster of trees got a foothold, let the sand pile up over the years, then grew more trees on top of that, and have the cycle repeat for generations.

Finn figured that's what had happened to create the "bluffs" that rose beside the lagoon. Finn guessed the natural path between the water's edge and the tall grasses of the marsh must be maintained by the large pony population using it to get further inland from the wash he had just come up.

The sandy path rose gently out of the marshland and

wound its way to the back of the forested hill behind the bluffs.

Within seconds the path went from sandy grass and sun to covered in pine needles and shaded by the stunted pine forest. Finn breathed in the fresh scent and took in the hardened sentinels that made the hill possible.

While stunted, the pines were still tall enough to allow him to walk under most of the boughs without much problem. He noticed the ground cover, thin in the constant shade, left an unobstructed view through the trees and over the marsh to the vibrant blue ocean waters.

As he walked along the edge of the small forest where the land fell away into the marsh below, Finn was careful not to get too close to the drop off in case the ground wasn't as solid as it looked. He took a few minutes to enjoy the elevated view, even if it was only ten feet up.

He closed his eyes once again, focused his power, and sensed the large deposit of precious metals to his left, not far away.

He opened his eyes and breathed in a lungful of salty air before turning and slowly making his way through the trees, taking his time and enjoying the shade of the trees.

After a few dozen yards, the forest parted to reveal a small meadow with lush green grass covering the suddenly firm ground, and three huge trees in the center. The air had changed as well, still holding a hint of ocean salt, but now the smell of grass and loam filled his nostrils.

Finn frowned and turned to make sure he hadn't stepped through a portal by accident, but the pine forest still stood behind him. He turned back and noticed that the three large trees growing in the center of the meadow were oaks, not pines like the rest of the forest. The thick-trunked trees grew in a triangle, equidistant from one another, and towered a good fifty feet overhead, their thick green canopies shading a large swath of ground around the bases of the oaks.

Finn decided there was something very odd about this place. Considering that three fifty-foot-tall trees would be visible for miles on the ridiculously flat barrier island, Finn found it impossible to believe he hadn't noticed them at all until stumbling into them. He knew there must be magic involved somehow, but it was either so subtle that he couldn't detect it, or it just didn't affect him for some reason, so there was nothing for him to sense.

He definitely felt that there a huge amount of treasure close by, and he guessed it must be buried at the center of those three trees.

Finn sighed, reached around, and pulled the foldable camping shovel he had bought on his second trip out for Penny from a side pocket in the backpack.

He unfolded the short shovel blade and frowned. "Why is this never easy?"

He marched over to the trees, dropped his pack, fell to his knees, and jammed the shovel into the ground. To his surprise, he only had to dig about six inches down before he hit something solid. Two minutes of clearing the dirt and widening the hole later, Finn pulled a small iron-bound chest from the dirt. After setting it down beside him, he brushed off the soil and flipped the latch.

The chest was full of gold coins. He picked one up to examine more closely and saw that it was a Spanish doubloon.

"Man, this is like the seventh treasure made up of Spanish gold I've found. How the hell did they not go broke losing all this money all the time?"

He looked around, feeling a bit odd that nothing had attacked him so far, and saw that the coast was clear. With a shrug, he began moving the coins from the chest into his pack. He was careful not to overload it after the talk he and Mila had had about Penny's concerns that he would hurt himself empowering his body with magic in order to carry so much. Normally he would argue that they were worrying too much, but he respected their opinions, and he had to admit that he was not always the best judge of what he should and shouldn't do. Besides, he had a good ten- or twelve-mile hike down the beach to get back to town. There was only so much his body could take while hauling two thousand pounds of gold on his back, so he kept it down to a half-ton.

As he pulled out the third chest, he finally heard what he had been waiting for.

A branch snapped close behind him. He started to spin around, reaching for the front of his Speedo, but a club smashed into the side of his head and knocked him to the ground.

To his attacker's surprise, the hit didn't knock him out. They jumped back in fear as he sprang to his feet and roared.

The roar faded, and his eyes widened when he saw that his attackers were five naked and skittish men and women.

He looked the closest man—the one still holding the club—up and down but stopped and stared at the man's feet. Or not feet, hooves… He stopped and stared at the man's hooves.

"What the fuck?"

"Goddammit, Harry!" the park ranger from the beach yelled as she stepped into the clearing and marched towards them.

"Ranger? Who are your naked friends?" Finn asked, a grin on his face.

She narrowed her eyes, then flipped a hand his way. "Sleep."

Finn closed his eyes and tipped over backward, slamming into the ground like a felled tree.

Soon after, the meadow rumbled with his snores.

CHAPTER TWENTY-ONE

A million swarming black flies slammed into a lower-level side door of the factory at full speed, causing no harm whatsoever to the door or the surrounding structure. The resulting explosion from the four wards closest to the flies blew chunks of cinderblock out into the empty tarmac surrounding the building while at the same time vaporizing about fifty pounds of common housefly.

It also set off an alarm that screeched through the interior of the building, drawing every occupant's attention and causing a mad rush of Rougarou and thrall towards the now destroyed door.

Yaminah froze, her fist cocked back to deliver another blow to the limp, hanging form of Victoria, who mumbled something about getting free in a pain-induced delirium.

Yaminah narrowed her eyes and glared daggers at Victoria. "Is this your doing?"

If Victoria did attempt to say something, it just came out as unintelligible babble along with a stream of fresh blood that splattered on the floor to add to the already sizable puddle.

Yaminah pushed her away in disgust before running toward the breach, leaving Victoria to swing and twist alone in the dim factory.

The relief of not being worked over was too much for the Valkyrie, and her head dropped to her chest as she passed out.

Mila pulled her awareness from the fly she had been using to see when Yaminah joined the other minions and gave the signal they were clear to go in.

Next to a different door, Jenny hit the button of a detonator remote and three shaped magical charges went off, causing a barely audible popping sound, followed by a sizzling purple puff of smoke as magical acid was blasted out of the charges to burn through the door hinges in half a second. The job done, the acid evaporated into the aether as the heavy metal door fell out of its fame.

Carl caught the door before it hit the ground and gently laid it down, then signaled Howard to move in.

The giant orc made a fist, cracking the knuckles of one hand while holding a pair of bolt cutters in the other, and stepped over the door. Jenny moved in behind him, a satchel full of explosive traps over her shoulder. Remmy went next, her daggers held in a reverse grip, followed by Mila, who held Gram extended in one hand. Finally Carl, his rifle to his shoulder, stepped through to cover their rear.

Once inside, after checking that the area was clear, the team got to their assignments. Mila moved up beside Howard as Jenny sprinted across the room, her elven foot falls unnaturally quiet, and begin placing traps at key choke points.

"Go," Carl whispered to Mila. "Tina and Nick are set. I'll cover our exit."

She gave him a nod and stepped between a steel form-press and a stack of molding crates to head deeper into the factory, Remmy and Howard close on her heels.

Mila led them through the old crates and machinery as quietly as she could, painfully aware of the time crunch they were under.

They rounded a bank of shelves, and Mila came eye to eye with a pair of unmoving thralls who either hadn't got the message that they were under attack or didn't care. She skipped to the side to avoid crashing into them and barely made it. Howard wasn't so lucky and crashed into the pair. The contact must have knocked something loose because both blank-faced men suddenly snarled and leaped at Howard's throat.

Mila's reaction speed surprised even her. Before the thralls could take a full step, she lashed out with Gram and removed both of their heads in a single stroke.

The bodies collapsed to the floor at Howard's feet. He and Mila's eyes met, and he gave her a nod of thanks.

Mila continued down the aisle and stepped out into the cleared central area of the factory floor to spot Victoria's still swinging body thirty feet further away.

"Looks clear." Howard scanned the dark corners.

A ripping sound tore through the air from the far side of the factory, followed by the sound of rushing air. Dust kicked up all over the factory and flew toward the corner where they had set up the distraction with the flies.

Remmy's duster flapped in the sudden wind, and they were all forced to turn their heads or have twenty years of dirt and dust blast them in the face.

Just as suddenly as it started, the wind stopped, to leave the air hazy with dust.

"What the fuck was that?" Mila hissed as she looked toward the source.

The two-story building-within-a-building where she and Remmy had run into the thralls the first time they had been there blocked her view. A flash of blue light and a chest-thumping shockwave tossed dozens of broken thralls and Rougarou in every direction from behind the inner building. The bodies slammed into the ceiling or the far wall beyond the factory floor, where they left blood splatters from the impacts.

"One of Jenny's gravity grenades," Howard took off at a jog towards Victoria. "Come on, we need to hurry. They don't have enough to hold that horde off for long."

Mila and Remmy took off after Howard, and Mila passed him at a run. She slid to a stop, to catch Victoria mid-swing and steady her body. Howard arrived, immediately lifted the bolt cutters, and got them between one of the shackles and Victoria's swollen and bloody hands. He wasn't being careful, opting for a quick escape.

Mila cringed when Victoria's wrist was bent at an odd angle so he could get the blade into place. He pulled the handles together, straining with everything he had until a vein popped out on his forehead from the effort, but the shackles didn't so much as flex. He pulled the blade out and decided to just cut the chain, and deal with the shackles later, but the chain had the same resistance.

"What the fuck is this shit made of?" Howard readjusted the cutters.

When he moved the cutter blade, it scraped across the chain link, sending out black sparks of magical energy.

"Infernal magic?" Mila bit her lip. "They must have some sort of reinforcement woven into them."

An idea hit her. She held out her hands for the cutters. "Let me try something."

Howard gave her sidelong glance but handed over the red-handled bolt cutters without a word.

"Yeah, I know." She rolled her eyes. "Just give me a sec."

Mila had been able to infuse her body with celestial magic to enhance her reflexes and strength, so why not an inanimate object? The concept made sense to her, but she didn't know if the magic would bind to something mundane or if it had to be alive. The shackles weren't alive but were very obviously infused, so it should work for her too.

She focused on the cutters, and channeled a stream of power into them, willing it to reinforce and empower the cutter blades. At first, the magic just kind of pooled in her hands, not knowing what to do next, but with some forceful direction on her part, the power finally made the jump from her to the cutter handles. Once the connection was made, the power rushed from her at an alarming rate. Her eyes snapped open, and she saw that the blades of the long-handled cutters glowed with golden light that grew in intensity as more and more magic flowed into them.

Mila cut off the flow, a gut feeling telling her that she could put so much power into the cutter that it would eventually destroy the metal blades and release all that power in one go. Not something she wanted to experience.

As soon as she stopped feeding power, the light dimmed rapidly. Evidently, the cutters couldn't hold it, so it just evaporated. Maybe the craftsmanship could become a factory to permanently imbue things with magic; she would have to have a conversation with Penny about it later. Right now, she needed to get Victoria free.

"I can't reach the shackles, and I can't hand the cutters off to you without them losing the charge I gave them," Mila turned her back to a slack-jawed Howard and lifted her arms. "I need you to lift me up so I can cut the shackles myself."

He put his massive hands around her waist and squeezed tightly to lift her a good four feet off the ground and give her plenty of height to get at the double set of shackles.

As she wedged the blade under the first shackle, a gold and black spark popped as the residual magic in the blade reacted with the infernal magic in the metal.

Mila channeled power into the cutters again and forced the handles together with everything she had. Being held up didn't give her much leverage, but she discovered she didn't need much.

As soon as the blade began to glow, a shower of black and gold sparks flew from the metal, and with minimal effort, she cut through the cuff.

Mila pumped a fist in victory, and whispered a quiet, "Yes!" before moving to the next cuff, which came off just as easy as the first, though Mila did notice burn marks on Victoria's pale and bloody skin.

The next set of cuffs actually held up her unconscious body, so working the blade between the metal and skin ended up stabbing the blade into the swollen skin of Victoria's hand. Mila gritted her teeth and pushed it in until she had enough to cut through in one go, then channeled magic and pulled the handles closed.

The cuff popped off, and Victoria's arm, along with her entire left side, fell, now that her body wasn't being suspended evenly. When all that weight slammed down, Mila heard a loud pop from Victoria's right hand as the thumb and a few bones in her hand broke under the stress. Her hand, now slimmer without the bones in the way, slipped from the cuff on its own.

Her body fell lifelessly to the ground.

Mila sucked in a breath, hoping Victoria's head hadn't hit the concrete floor. It would be a hell of a thing if they got to her, but she died from being freed.

Relief washed over Mila when she saw Remmy slide in and catch Victoria's head and shoulders in her lap.

Howard put Mila down, and she dropped to her knees to place a hand on Victoria's chest. As she had imbued the cutters, she forced healing magic into the broken Valkyrie.

It took a second and a lot of her power, but Victoria's eyes fluttered open and she looked around in confusion, then spotted Mila. A pained expression crossed her face.

"He caught you too?" she asked in a rasping voice that sounded nothing like the strong woman that Mila had gotten to know as her sister.

Mila shook her head. "Not if I can help it. We're here to rescue you, but you're in a bad way, Victoria. I need you to drink this, okay?" She pulled one of her healing potions from her corset and pulled the cork.

Victoria opened her mouth and Mila poured the red liquid in, letting her swallow once before pouring the rest.

Victoria swallowed hard and looked up with tears in her eyes. "I didn't think anyone was coming. I thought I was going to die. Actual death." She coughed, and blood spattered out onto the floor.

"You're okay. The healing potion will kick in in a second." Mila stroked Victoria's blood-soaked hair out of her face.

"This is going to suck," Victoria groaned, before clenching her teeth as the potion kicked in, and the bones in her hand and toe began to set themselves with loud popping and crunching sounds.

An explosion roared from the far end of the factory, but this time it was out on the factory floor. Mila looked over her shoulder to see Carl and Jenny running her way as a horde of Rougarou raced around the corner after them. Another explosion blew five of the tightly packed wolfmen to bloody chunks as they passed over a tripwire Jenny had set up.

"We have to go!" Carl shouted and waved, all pretext of stealth abandoned in the face of the charging monsters behind him.

Victoria let out a cry as the healing potion did its painful work. Mila scrambled to her feet, grabbed Victoria under the arms and began to drag her to the cover of the maze of crates and machinery. Remmy took one of her arms to help pull while the team opened up with spells and silenced gunfire.

"They overran our first way out, head for the second egress point," Carl ordered, calmly laying round after round into the oncoming Rougarou.

Mila nodded, even though he couldn't see her, and began dragging Victoria towards two particularly large machines that formed an alley between them that butted up against an outer wall.

A black bolt of magical return fire hit Jenny in the thigh, knocking her to the ground. Carl kept firing with one hand and reached down to grip the back of Jenny's collar and drag her while still firing. Jenny opened her bag and pulled out a healing potion, downing it quickly before selecting a glass orb filled with a green liquid. She cocked her arm, ready to throw but waited for the most opportune time.

Carl got them around the corner and picked up his speed, dragging Jenny at a slow jog. Howard was still out in the open, slinging spell after spell and glancing down the aisle they retreated through to judge how far to let them get before taking cover himself.

Mila heard Yaminah let out a scream of anger before three of the black diamond-shaped missiles came at Howard's chest. He was able to put up a bubble that deflected two of them, but the third hit him in the left shoulder and exploded. His shirt was shredded at the impact site and green blood sprayed against a pillar behind the orc, but the pain didn't seem to register as he continued to send bubble after bubble from his right hand.

On judging the rest of them had moved far enough, Howard broke off and sprinted down the aisle, to catch up with Carl and Jenny. He reached down and took over dragging duty while Carl took aim as he walked backward.

The horde crested the corner, Rougarou leading the pack, but thralls mixed in as well, their jerking motions gone now that they had a target in sight.

Jenny threw the glass orb.

It tumbled through the air and looked like she had thrown it too high and was going to miss the leading enemies. Carl, however, took aim in a move they must have practiced many times to pull off as flawlessly as they did.

A muffled shot rang out and the glass orb exploded, the green contents fanning out and letting off black smoke. In the blink of an eye, the liquid burst into flame as it rained down on the charging Rougarou and thralls.

The front line went down, howling in pain as the caustic liquid not only seemed to burn, but acted as an acid as well, dissolving any flesh it touched.

"Nice shot," Jenny chuckled, holding up a fist that Carl bumped.

"Let's go," Howard said, downing a healing potion with one hand while he began dragging Jenny again. "That's not going to hold them back for long."

Smoke and flame filled the aisle, the heat so intense that it peeled the paint from the machinery. A figure walked through the flames and came to stand in front of the horde as if she hadn't even noticed the fire and acid that was holding back the rest of her fighters.

"You're right," Yaminah growled. "It won't."

CHAPTER TWENTY-TWO

Yaminah slashed at the burning ground with her left hand. A black wave of magic fanned out and smothered the flames, revealing the gathered thralls and Rougarou eager to get back to the hunt.

As she pointed a finger at Carl, Yaminah smiled. "Leave the Valkyries, but the others are fair game."

The horde rushed forward, talons extended and teeth bared.

Howard shot a bubble out of his fingers that zipped across the gap and morphed into a net made of thin silver wires that glinted in the light as it flew directly toward the disciple.

Yaminah waved her hand and a thrall was pulled from the ranks streaming past her, as if the hapless thrall had been pulled through the air by the hand of a god. The flailing husk of a person flew into the net to be wrapped up tight an instant before the fine mesh of wire crackled with blue arcs of electricity. The thrall hit the ground and flopped around like a fish out of water.

"Nice try," Yaminah said. "My turn."

She raised her hands to cast, but her eyes went wide when Carl, Howard, and Jenny all threw spells at once, then immediately switched to their guns, mowing down thralls and the occasional Rougarou by the dozens.

Yaminah threw up a shield to block the barrage of attack spells but was quickly lost in the pressing mass of bodies streaming past her.

Mila felt a hand on her arm and looked down to see Victoria's hard expression. "Let me up, the potion has done its work."

Mila and Remmy stopped pulling her and helped the tall woman to her feet. She kicked off her remaining heel and held out a hand. "I need a weapon."

"What do I fight with then?" Mila asked, a little surprised.

"You don't. You need to make an exit for us. My powers are pretty much drained, but for some reason, I can feel them returning even though you're standing right here. We should both be getting weaker by the second, but I'm not one to look a gift horse in the mouth. I may not have my powers, but I do have thousands of years' worth of experience."

Mila couldn't argue with the logic and handed Gram to her. "Don't lose that; it was a gift. Remmy, watch my back while I blow a hole in this place."

"You got it, boss." She had a wicked gleam in her eye that Mila hadn't ever seen before in the goblin, and suspected that she was secretly enjoying all this.

They had pulled themselves down the aisle far enough that they were now in an alcove created by two machines that were twenty feet long and made of solid steel, giving them relative protection in the ten-foot-wide space. Technically someone could come over the top of one of the machines, but it was unlikely in the next few seconds.

All Mila had to do was blow a hole in the cinder block wall. She pulled out the Ivar aimed it at the wall and pulled the trigger a couple of times. The drain on her magic when using the weapon had gone down considerably since she had first fired it, but it was still a good chunk of power, and she needed to not let her power management leave her vulnerable.

The two bolts of raw magic slammed into the concrete blocks, each one exploding in showers of black and gold sparks, but leaving nothing more than two small chips for all the bluster.

"Oh, fuck," Mila breathed, putting the pistol back in its holster and running up to the wall. She placed a hand on it and felt the infernal power radiating through it, bolstering its durability.

The spell felt very similar to what Carl had done to the walls of the bar in Elk River. The difference was that this spell was powered with infernal magic. A lot of infernal magic. Mila didn't have enough power to cancel out what had been imbued in the wall. She needed a plan, and she needed it two minutes ago.

As she turned back to the fight, Mila saw that Jenny's and Howard's potions had finally kicked in and they were both back in fighting shape. The three G.A.E.L. team members were efficient and deadly using a combination of magic and tech, and hours of practice together had turned them into a well-oiled fighting machine. Where they let some through, Remmy would appear and dispatch the enemy with her two long daggers before vanishing again.

The real MVP was Victoria. She had waded into the enemies and now laid waste to them with graceful sword and foot movements. She would also occasionally use one of the enemies as a shield by throwing thralls into attackers, or hold them at arm's length and let their comrades rip them to pieces while she took care of others at the end of Gram.

Despite Victoria's claim that she didn't have enough magic left to fight effectively with magic, Mila could see that she had empowered her muscles and reflexes, if just a bit. She would get out of the way of a set of talons just in time, then pick up a fully grown man turned thrall and throw him ten feet through the air to crash into more thralls.

She had cleared out a hole to fight in and took on attackers from all angles. That gave the G.A.E.L. team a little room to breathe, and they were slowly chipping away at the massive numbers, but Mila could see that the only reason they hadn't been overrun was that they had funneled the enemy down so that their huge numbers didn't mean a whole lot.

Watching Victoria fight gave Mila an idea. She searched quickly for a suitable tool for the job. At the base of the machine on her right was a five-gallon bucket with scraps of metal in it. A quick search and she found a foot-long section of steel tubing that would work.

She turned back to the wall and put her hand on it to feel how the reinforcement spell was woven into the structure. After a few seconds, she could begin to see the pattern in the wall. It was like a webbed lattice with the intersections of the lines of power acting as anchor points. If she took out an anchor point, then the power lines around it wouldn't be stable enough and might disintegrate, but if she could cut off a whole section from the main lattice, then that whole section would go down.

The lattice was in a diamond shape, with each anchor being about a foot from the next. If she could destroy nine points, she could open up a pretty large hole for them to get through.

She didn't have to overpower the whole system, she just had to overpower nine little points. That was completely doable.

She held the pipe in her fist so she could stab it at the wall, then channeled power into it. The end of the pipe gave off a shimmering golden light. With a little magic to enhance her strength, she found the first spot and stabbed the pipe into it. There was a flash of black and gold as the opposing magics fought one another, but her power far outstripped the single node. After a second's resistance, the pipe rammed two inches into the concrete block.

A quick check told her that it had worked; the node was gone, and the lattice around it had faded as well.

"Only eight more to go," she yelled as a battle cry, slamming the pipe into the next node.

She continued, using up her magic at a prodigious rate, but getting results. A quick glance over her shoulder and she could see that the team had cleared out the enemy between them and Victoria, letting her focus more on the fight in front of her while they supported her at range.

Mila could see the faint outline of large wings coming

from Victoria's back. They were barely visible and made completely of light, but Mila wondered why they showed at all. Shouldn't she be conserving her power? Unless the wings were something else, like a reaction to circumstance, maybe? Mila shook her head. She didn't have time for this.

She stabbed the next node, and it went out much easier than the first two. The fourth was even easier. It was still taking a considerable amount of power, but it did confirm that the entire structure was weakening with each node removed. She continued punching the pipe into the wall, and in a few seconds, she had the wall cleared of the reinforcement spell.

She took a step back, pulled out the Ivar, and aimed at the wall once again. "Let's try this again, shall we?"

She pulled the trigger to send a single bolt at the wall. This time when it hit, there were no black sparks. Instead, the bolt exploded and sent chips of hot concrete flying, but more importantly, it left a hole a foot in diameter.

Mila grinned and blasted away at the wall. By the time she had a hole large enough to run thorough, she had a splitting headache and felt like she'd hit the bottom of the tank magically.

"Let's go, people!" Mila sent a bolt from the Ivar into the horde, cutting down several of the enemies in one shot, but her vision started to blur as her head screamed in pain. She slipped the pistol back into its holster.

"Go! I'll hold them off while you get out, then I'll follow!" Victoria's face and clothes didn't seem nearly as bloody as Mila would have guessed, considering the piles of bodies around her.

Jenny grabbed her satchel and ran through the opening,

rummaging in the bag as she went. Howard followed, sending one last bubble that morphed into a spinning blade that sliced a Rougarou in half at the waist.

Mila looked past Victoria and saw that Yaminah had climbed up onto a worktable and watched the retreat with a sour look on her face, but did nothing to stop them. Mila would have thought she would be throwing spells left and right, but it seemed like she had just given up. Carl and Remmy made it out, and it was just Mila and Victoria left.

"Come on, we're clear, Victoria. Let's get the fuck out of here."

Veronica took a quick look back, then went back to fighting, timing her run with a lull in the fight.

The blood drained from Mila's face when she saw a black void rip open in the main section of the factory behind Yaminah.

"We have to go now!" Mila shouted, waving for her sister to follow.

Mila decided she could take the pain if it meant not having to fight Azoth right now and pulled the Ivar back out.

She shot a bolt into the group right in front of Victoria to give her the opening she needed to disengage. The tall woman turned and sprinted towards Mila and the exit.

Two steps away from Mila, Victoria's expression went from determined to panicked to pained as she doubled over and fell to the floor. Gram also skittered to a stop at Mila's feet.

Mila had no idea what had just happened, but when she looked past the charging thralls, she could see what had gone wrong.

Azoth had returned. Slung over his shoulder was an unconscious woman that Mila suspected was the Lone Valkyrie he had left to collect that morning. Victoria had been so weakened that when she appeared, it took the last of what Victoria had and put her down.

Mila didn't have time to pull Victoria out before the thralls would be upon them, and if she stayed to fight, Azoth would join the battle and it would all be over.

It was an impossible situation, but if she had a choice, it was to fight. It was always to fight. Because if you didn't fight, you couldn't win.

Mila hooked her foot under Gram's blade and kicked it up in front of her. With magically enhanced reflexes, she snatched it out of the air by the handle and dove into the oncoming thrall.

"Halt!"

Azoth's shout shook the windows, and every one of his minions froze in their tracks. Even Yaminah stood stock still.

The sudden silence was disorienting, and Mila began to back away while Azoth tried to figure out what the hell was going on. He spotted her and pointed a stony hand, as the void in his hood seemed to darken with anger.

"You! You will halt!"

Mila gave him the finger.

She glanced down to see that Victoria was awake, but not able to do much more than groan in pain.

The odds were far too in Azoth's favor right now. What Mila needed was a miracle.

Then, to Mila's surprise, a miracle stepped out of the portal behind Azoth.

Missy, dressed in a super short pleated plaid miniskirt, thigh-high black combat boots, and a hooded back t-shirt, looked like she was ready to eat a frying pan and spit out nails. Her blue pigtails shook with rage, and she had a twisted snarl of anger on her face as she stared daggers at the back of Azoth's hood.

Mila smiled. Now they might *just* have a chance.

CHAPTER TWENTY-THREE

Mila opened her mouth to shout something at Azoth to let Missy know she had sisters in the fight with her, but Missy beat her to it.

"This is unacceptable, Azoth!" Missy shouted, her fists clenched. "You are exceeding the terms of our deal..." Her voice trailed off when she realized there was something more important happening.

Mila's eyes widened in shock as she and Missy locked gazes. They just stared at one another while Mila's mind ran at a thousand miles an hour.

Missy had made a deal with the Drude? They were on friendly enough terms that she felt comfortable using his portal, and shouting at him in his own lair? What the fuck was happening? How long had it been happening?

A million more questions flashed through her mind, but Mila knew she wasn't going to get any answers right now. Nothing had changed. She still needed to get out and take Victoria with her more than ever now.

"Yaminah," Azoth sneered in his creaking voice, "Missy. Bring me those two. I wish to feast."

Mila realized it was much worse than just some deal when Missy physically tried to resist, and her chest flared with black infernal magic as she cried out before locking her jaw. She glared daggers at Mila.

"Why couldn't you just do what you were told?" Missy coiled her legs and leaped from the ground onto a table, then sprinted towards Mila.

Mila grabbed the front of Victoria's blouse and dragged her toward the opening behind her.

Fully enhanced with magic, Missy's limbs glowed with golden light as she raced across another workbench then leaped over the tightly packed minions to land ten feet in front of Mila, already sprinting and cocking her fist back to deliver a magically enhanced punch.

There was a wet squishing noise and Missy slammed to a halt, her body doubling over and lifting into the air before falling back to her feet.

There was a rush of air as Remmy appeared, kneeling in front of Missy, the butt of a broken broom handle jammed into the floor and the broken end poking out of Missy's back.

Yaminah landed behind Missy, her hands coming up to blast Mila, but her eyes widened and she hastily threw up a shield as firebolts and ice spikes shot past Mila, followed by rapid-fire silenced rifle rounds. They slammed into Yaminah's shield and blew her off her feet.

Howard knelt beside Mila and scooped Victoria up in his arms. "Thought we should come see what was keeping you."

Mila threw up a shield to block a set of the three diamond missiles from Yaminah. They ricocheted into the wall overhead to explode and send chips of concrete raining down.

Missy screamed in rage, the shock of being stabbed fading away. Quick as a cat, she backhanded Remmy in the chest, sending the small goblin flying into Mila, who dropped her shield and caught her.

Mila put her shield back up and quickly backed toward the hole.

"Do not let her escape!" Azoth roared.

The previously frozen minions sprang into action, sprinting past Yaminah to block her line of sight and ability to cast any more spells at Mila. Missy was busy pulling the makeshift spear from her abdomen, so Mila dropped her shield, turned, and ran out into the light of day.

It took her eyes a second to adjust, and she nearly tripped over an elongated black box that lay in front of the opening. As she scrambled over it, Mila wondered who would leave a box out in the open like that, until she saw Jenny's maniacal smile as she pressed the button of a remote detonator.

The black box flipped open and shot hundreds of ball bearings out in rapid succession. The speed the projectiles flew from the box kept increasing until a continuous stream pelted the concrete bricks and zinged into the opening, eliciting screams and howls of pain.

The accumulated hits and the weakened state of the wall's reinforcement spell finally hit the breaking point, and the wall collapsed to block the enemy.

There were still other ways they could get out of the building, so Mila and the rest of the team ran for all they were worth, ducked through the hole in the fence they had cut on the way in and piled into the van Nick had pulled to the curb once his and Tina's part of the rescue was over.

Carl pulled the door closed. "We're in. Let's get out of here, Nick."

"You got it." Nick stepped on the gas and had them around the corner in a matter of seconds.

"Well, that was exciting!"

CHAPTER TWENTY-FOUR

Penny added her own infusion of magic to the glowing bubble that hovered six inches above the reclaimed wooden table. She glanced down at the sketch for reference, then mentally forged the part while Lance and Rebecca fed in extra power to keep the form solid.

Each of the twenty-odd parts took a lot of power to create since they were designed to hold more magical charge than was normally imbued into objects, and they needed to be made of sturdier stuff than anything that could be forged or machined.

The power flowing out of Penny was substantial enough that she needed to refuel after each part they created.

After putting the finishing touches on the oddly shaped part, Penny checked to be sure it was perfect. Not seeing any problems, she willed the object into existence and the bubble popped. The vaguely boat-shaped part dropped to the table with a solid sound thunk.

With a whoosh of exhaustion, Penny sat back on her

haunches and picked up the heavy part to examine it closely before she set it beside the row of parts they had created over the last few hours.

"Only a dozen more to go," Lance said with a laugh. "Does anyone want a drink? I think I could use a drink."

"That sounds wonderful, honey." Rebecca stretched her arms above her head and sharply twisted her torso to pop all the vertebrae from her tail bone to her shoulder blades in one go.

"Oh, god. That felt great!" She rolled her head around her shoulders.

"Penny, you want anything? We have beer, wine, and a full bar. What sounds good?" Lance rolled open a garage door-style cabinet to reveal a fully stocked bar.

"Seriously," Rebecca stage-whispered to Penny, "he's an amazing mixologist. Don't tell him I said so. He doesn't need a bigger head than he already has."

She winked at Lance, and he laughed.

"It's a byproduct of my potion-mixing. Basically the same thing." He shrugged shyly, embarrassed by the praise.

Rebecca laughed. "Yeah, because all potion makers want their concoctions not only to be effective but to taste good as well. That's a normal thing. Oh wait, no, it's not. You're exceptional, babe. Just accept it."

Lance pulled out a couple of bottles and filled a shaker with ice. "If you say so, babe. I like to think that I'm just doing it properly."

"So, instead of thinking you're an exceptional potion maker, you would rather think that all the other potion makers are just doing it wrong?"

The slack-jawed look of shocked realization on Lance's face made Rebecca and Penny burst out laughing.

"That's not what I meant," he tried to argue, but he just ended up laughing along with them. "Okay, okay. Now that we all know I'm actually a low-key potion snob, what can I get you, Penny? Becca and I usually have a daiquiri on a warm afternoon like today, but I can make you anything you like."

"Squee shi? *Like a frozen daiquiri you get at a resort?*" Penny tossed a few mixed nuts into her mouth.

Nuts were some of the densest food they had on hand to help her replenish her magic. Luckily, they had a lot of nuts in the pantry. So far, Penny had eaten six bowls of the salty treats in order to replenish what she had used in making the first half of the device's parts. After Lance had filled the third bowl, he'd just left the bag on the table, to Penny's relief.

"Like a frozen..." The look of disgust on Lance's face made Penny's eye ridges rise in alarm. "You poor thing. What kind of monsters are you drinking with? That's it, I'm making you a daiquiri. End of discussion."

Rebecca laughed and picked a cashew out of the mixed nuts. "You tell her, babe."

Penny watched as Lance poured light rum, lime juice, and simple syrup into the shaker, then put the top on, hit it with the heel of his hand to secure it, and shook it vigorously for nearly a full minute. While shaking away, he opened one of the cabinets that turned out to be a large freezer faced to look like the rest of the cabinets, pulled three chilled coupe glasses out, and set them on the counter. After removing the lid from the shaker, he strained a frothy off-white concoction nearly to the rim of each glass. With a twist of lime peel in each, he carefully brought two over to the table and served one to each of them before returning for his own.

Lance sat and held up his coupe in a salute.

"Cheers," he announced, then took a sip and smacked his lips.

Penny sniffed the concoction. Not surprisingly, it smelled of lime, but there was a real sweetness to the lime that made her mouth water. Not wanting the spill the extremely full drink, she lowered her head to the glass and sipped from the rim.

Her eyes widened as the perfect balance of sweet and tart hit her tongue, followed quickly by the earthy spice of the rum.

"Good, isn't it?" Rebecca took a sip of her own.

Penny nodded in answer as she took another sip right away.

"It's your new favorite drink, isn't it?" Lance said with just a touch of smugness.

Penny nodded again. It really was one of the most delicious drinks she had ever had. Finn and Mila would love them. She would have to make some for them when she got home. She was pretty sure they had all the ingredients at the condo already.

Looking between Lance and Rebecca and their happy, content faces, Penny had to smile.

"Chi chi, chiri shee. *You two remind me of Finn and Mila. Comfortable with each other while not demanding anything more than you should of one another. It's nice to see that they aren't the only ones out there who figured it out."* Penny smiled at their happiness.

Rebecca cocked her head to the side and raised an eyebrow. "Who are Finn and Mila?"

Penny didn't know what to say for a few seconds. She had forgotten that as far as Rebecca and Lance were concerned, Penny was the one who needed a device to fight and kill a Drude.

Penny reconsidered that maybe these two were not so much happy, as just insane. Who helps a random dragon build a powerful magical artifact just because they asked nicely? Finn would, that's who. Mila might ask a question of two, but she would help too.

Penny chuckled and dove into the tale of how she and Finn had met, adding detail when they asked for clarification, and drawing out the tale.

They finished their break, and Penny was still telling them about some adventure before her and Finn ever got to Earth. She realized this was going to be the long version of the story.

They had created three more parts and had a couple more daiquiris before she got to the part where they defeated the Dark Star and Mila realized she was a Valkyrie.

Rebecca stopped the tale with a raised hand. "Wait, Mila is a Valkyrie?"

Penny nodded as she chomped on a handful of nuts.

"But you said she's a Doctor of Anthropology. What is she, some kind of super genius?"

Penny narrowed her eyes and cocked her head. "Skee chi.

Chi? *I mean, she's pretty smart, but I wouldn't say she's a genius. I mean, maybe in some vague technical sense you could argue, that is, but in reality, she's just a smart and capable person. Why?*"

"How old was she when she awoke to being a Valkyrie?"

Penny shrugged. "Squee? Shiri see squee. *Like thirty. Thirty-two? Actually, I've never asked her how old she is; age isn't a concern to dragons. We live for so long, it doesn't matter to us.*"

"Am I missing some part of the timeline?" Rebecca shook her head slightly. "When did this fight with the Dark Star happen?"

"Chi. *Five or six months ago.*" Penny frowned, not sure what Rebecca was getting at.

Rebecca returned the frown, then opened the old book her ancestor Gregory had written about his time with the Valkyries. "That's so weird that she awoke so late. It's very well documented that it happens right around the end of puberty. Who did she end up being?"

"Shee shee. *She's Mila. That's it. She hasn't had any other lives yet.*"

"She's a *new* Valkyrie?" Rebecca sat up straight and flipped pages excitedly. "I can't believe this. Okay, where is it? Here it is!"

She read the passage while Penny's eyes grew wide with surprise.

"Right here. Okay, Gregory asked specifically about how Valkyries were born, but all the elder knew was that they would spontaneously pop into existence every few thousand years. She also said it hadn't happened in her lifetime that she knew about." Rebecca looked a Penny with a "holy shit" look then continued.

"It gets really interesting later, though. Gregory isn't satisfied with that vague answer and eventually seeks out the librarian at Alexandria. He explains that he's a historian and that he's trying to compile a complete compendium of the races and asks if they had any information on new Valkyries, and son of a bitch, they had a whole book on the subject."

Rebecca was becoming animated as she summed up what Gregory had found at the library.

"According to this book, which by the way was written by a Valkyrie, which goes against their typical secret society thing they have going on. Anyway, according to her, Valkyries are a product of the universe's desire to fall towards entropy; you know the whole heat death of the universe?"

Penny nodded, then stuffed more nuts in her mouth.

"Okay, well, if the universe needs to get to a place where everything is evenly divided out until there's nothing left, then things need to be balanced. According to the author, she believes the entire race of the Valkyries is a direct balancing act, by the universe, to even out the Drude.

"We know the Drude were the first to appear, then the Valkyries followed a few thousand years later, but no one knows where either of them actually come from. But, the idea that Valkyries are somehow a specially designed counter of power to the Drude comes from the fact that 'newborn' Valkyries thrown into unique situations that traditionally their kind didn't have a way to fight have been known to develop powers unique to them in order to overcome their particular situation.

"But even more interesting is the fact that those new powers are usually an adaptation of those around them, the evolutionary theory being that if the "locals" can survive, they must be onto something.

"I can't believe there is a new Valkyrie on Earth. She must have some incredible abilities considering her boyfriend is a Dwarf King."

"Shir chi? *Why does Finn being a royal matter?*"

Rebecca laughed with glee. "Because Dwarf Kings are incredibly magical. Almost on par with dragons. Actually, that's a bit much; nothing living is as magical as dragons. But I would argue they're on a par with unicorns. People *want* to follow them, even if they *say* otherwise. When the shit hits the fan, everyone lines up behind the Dwarf King. That doesn't mean they are good rulers or even good people; it just means that they hold power over people whether they want to or not.

"And now there's a new Valkyrie who is subconsciously soaking up every advantage she can get, and she just so happens to be trained by and sleeping with one of the most influential creatures in the universe."

Rebecca laughed and shook her head in disbelief. "Between Mila's ability to assimilate powers and traits and Finn's potent lineage, I would be shocked if Mila doesn't end up with a little dwarf in her DNA. I have to meet her someday. Promise me you'll introduce us. I have so many questions for her."

Penny was thunderstruck by all the information but nodded to Rebecca. She would definitely bring Finn and Mila to meet them, if for no other reason than to experience Lance's mixing abilities.

As she thought back to all the new abilities Mila was beginning to show, Penny could see a lot of Finn in them.

She had to wonder if this whole Fate thing Finn was always going on about mightn't really be a thing.

Penny shrugged. Life would be interesting either way.

CHAPTER TWENTY-FIVE

Nick slowed the van down now that they had a few blocks and several turns between them and the factory full of horrors. The farther away they got, the better Victoria got as the distance between her and the Lone Valkyrie Azoth had captured increased.

Mila sat on the floor of the van, Remmy's head in her lap as she groaned in pain. Tina opened a cabinet, pulled out a healing potion from a limited stash, and handed it to Mila.

"Thanks." Mila uncorked the vial and held it above Remmy's face. "Open up."

Remmy's eyes opened, saw the potion, and brightened. She opened wide and Mila poured the contents in, giving her time to swallow at the halfway point.

Gently stroking the goblin's green cheek, Mila smiled down at her. "You saved my life back there. Thanks."

Remmy gave a pained smile. "Just doing my job, boss. Although if you wanted to do me a favor..."

Mila chuckled. "Sure. What can I do for you?"

Remmy locked eyes with Mila and gave her a sad look. "If at all possible, could you take a shower soon? You smell like you last bathed in an alley."

Mila laughed a lot harder than the rest of them thought strictly necessary.

"Back at you, ya little shit."

A loud popping sound followed by a yelp from Remmy let everyone know that the potion was kicking in as her shoulder reset itself. The tight look of pain on her face quickly faded to a euphoric high as the magic in the potion released endorphins to cut down on the discomfort. After a few more seconds, she reached up and started scratching at her ribs as they healed.

Still a little high from the potion, she sat up and scooted across the floor to lean against the bench between Howard and Carl's knees. She pulled out her phone and buried her nose in it.

"Good talk," Mila said with a chuckle.

"Uh, is there someplace I should be heading?" Nick made a right turn onto a major thoroughfare. "I mean, I can just keep driving around, but I figure we need to make some plans and call in the cavalry to take care of that creepy Azoth guy. Not an easy thing to do crammed into a van."

Victoria finished a bottle of water Carl had given her. "I have a condo here in the city. We can go there."

"Won't Missy know about it? It would probably be the first place she comes looking for us." Mila didn't know how much control Azoth had over Missy, but if he could order her to attack, then he could just order her to find them.

Victoria shook her head as she finished off the water. "No one knows about this place. I use it to get away when I need to. None of the sisterhood has ever been there, and I used a fake name to buy it. We should be safe."

"We can set up some quick wards when we get there as well," Carl added.

"Okay, sounds good enough to me," Mila added.

Victoria gave Nick the address then turned back to Mila. "Do you have your phone? Mine was broken when I got captured."

Mila nodded, unzipped one of the pockets in the moto jacket, and handed the phone to her. "How did you get captured?"

"I thought I had made a mistake." She sighed. "But now I realize Missy set me up. She had me go check on one of our Lone Sisters, but as soon as I walked in, Azoth and Yaminah were waiting for me. They jumped me from behind. We struggled, but Azoth quickly pinned me to the wall with his fucking tentacles and Yaminah slapped the shackles on me. Once I was cut off from my magic, she hit me with a sleeping spell. Next thing I knew, I woke up hanging in that factory."

"I don't understand why she's doing this," Mila growled in frustration.

"I don't either. I've known Missy in one form or another for thousands of years. She's been fighting the Drude longer than most of us, but now she's feeding her sisters to our sworn enemy. I really don't get it."

"I don't know if this helps," Remmy said, holding out her phone to Mila, "but I found her Facebook page."

Mila took the phone and saw a profile picture that

was not at all what she expected. Instead of the blue-haired goth girl, it was a school photo of a brown-haired smiling girl in a private school blazer. If she hadn't known it was Missy, she wouldn't have looked twice, but now that she did, she could pick out the facial features easily.

With a frown, she handed the phone to Victoria. "What the hell? How did you find her?"

"Well, turns out I'm a clever goblin." Remmy smiled smugly. "I started under the assumption that there was no way a fifteen-year-old girl from SoCal didn't have a social media account somewhere. It was ridiculous to think she didn't, so I just looked up every girl born fifteen years ago named Missy Walker living in SoCal. When I didn't see her there, I knew she was lying about something. If that was her name, I was shit out of luck, but I guessed it was her age. There is no way she's younger than fifteen, so she had to be older. I just kept stepping back the age until I found her."

"Wait, you believed she was lying about her age before you believed she didn't have an account at all?" Carl asked.

"She's a fifteen-year-old girl from SoCal!" Remmy shouted with exasperation. "It was guaranteed that she had a page somewhere."

"I concur," Howard chimed in.

"Thank you!" Remmy held out her fist, and the orc bumped it with a wink.

"I mean, you found it, so you were right, but there are a lot of people who don't have social media," Carl said defensively.

"Yeah, old people," Remmy remarked under her breath.

"I don't have social media," Carl shot back. "Are you calling me old?"

Remmy looked up at him pursing her lips. "If the shoe fits…"

"You're one to talk, Remmy," Mila interjected. "You're older than Carl is."

Remmy crossed her arms with a pout. "Not in spirit, I'm not."

"I'll agree there," Jenny chimed in from the passenger seat. "Spiritually, Carl is about a hundred and fifty."

"You guys are the worst!" Carl crossed his arms and pouted.

"Was that all?" Mila tried to get the conversation back on track.

"Well, the last post is from five years ago. Evidently, she and her parents were in a car crash. Both parents died instantly, but she walked away without a scratch. My guess is that she really did awaken at fifteen, and that's how she survived the crash. But that was five years ago. She's twenty now but saying she's only fifteen. Granted, she is a young-looking twenty-year-old, but I think she started going goth so she could hide her age behind the makeup and clothes."

"But why?" Mila shook her head in confusion. "What was she doing for five years? I mean, she lost her family, but she had the sisterhood waiting for her, and instead, she spends five years alone? I don't get it."

"I think I know what she's trying to do." Victoria spoke quietly as she scrolled through the posts on Missy's page.

Mila scooted closer and saw picture after picture of Missy with her mom and dad, smiling and having fun together. The photos were interspersed with text images like "Family always has your back!" and "Stronger together :)" along with a picture of her and her mom lifting a huge cake they had just baked out of the oven.

"She's trying to go home," Victoria guessed.

Mila frowned. "How? There aren't any ships left on Earth. The Anthem was the last one, and Finn took care of it permanently. And why would her post history make you think that?"

Victoria sighed, then shut off the phone and handed it back to Remmy. "There are things we haven't told you about being a Valkyrie yet. I was waiting until you had a better understanding of why we are here at all, but now is as good a time as any.

"Being a Valkyrie has its perks. You won't age after a certain point, you have your powers, and you have a close group of people that you can call sister forever. But there are costs as well. One of the big ones is that we can't have children. Because of that, we grow very close with our birth families and cherish the family time we have with them because in the future, we will have to say goodbye, usually by disappearing before people notice that we aren't aging along with them.

"It's a pretty lonely existence in the end, but some Valkyries find a partner among their sisters—a person who will always be there, even after death. You can just find them again. It's a rare occurrence, though, so when it happens, it's cherished. Missy was one of the lucky ones who found a partner among our ranks. They have been married longer than most civilizations have existed, but when Missy took the assignment to transport," Victoria glanced at the other occupants and edited her words, "the object, she had to leave her wife at home. It was only supposed to be for a couple of hundred years for the whole mission, but *Earth* got stuck here, and now she's alone again.

"I think the death of her latest family was the last straw. She can't do this anymore."

"That's awful!" Mila tried to imagine what it would be like to be separated from Finn like that and shuddered. "But what does that have to do with joining the Drude?"

"Because the Drude are one of the few races that can travel through interstellar space without a ship, and they can take their thralls with them; it's how they invade other planets. I'm guessing they made a deal. She feeds him until he's strong enough to leave, and he takes her with him? I don't know." Victoria looked worn from the heaviness of the subject.

"What if she's going to give him the object?" Mila suggested.

Victoria shook her head sharply. "I don't care how far she's fallen; she would never do that. It would mean the destruction of everything she's trying to get back to. No, it's something else." She scrubbed her face with her hands. "It has to be something else."

"I hope you're right." Mila stroked Victoria's arm.

"I need to get the sisterhood moving. We need to cut Missy out before she can do any more damage." Victoria set her jaw with a new task to distract her. She opened the Valkyrie phone Mila had given her and dialed a number, then put the phone to her ear when it started ringing.

Mila pulled her knees to her chest and hoped she and

Finn wouldn't ever have to learn what it was like not to be there for one another. She smiled as she thought of him walking down the beach searching for treasure, like one of those old men with a metal detector.

She wondered what kind of swim trunks he took. Probably some kind of board shorts. She hoped it was board shorts. The last time they'd gone swimming together, he hadn't worn anything. While that was just fine with her, she was pretty sure the authorities would have something to say about it.

She really should have gone and bought him trunks just to be sure.

CHAPTER TWENTY-SIX

F inn awoke with a start, snorted, and sat up. He found himself in a domed subterranean cavern. The ground under him was more of the white sand he had been walking through all day, but the walls were a black rock that shimmered wetly in the flickering light of a fire.

The only way in or out of the cave seemed to be through a dark pool of water that took up half the floor space.

Reaching up to brush the hair out of his face, Finn found that he was wearing a pair of handcuffs. They looked like a regular pair of cuffs a cop would have...or a park ranger.

Finn frowned and got up onto his knees, to see a campfire burning. The tanned little park ranger sat on a log and poked the fire with a stick.

Movement caught his attention. He looked over to see the five naked, hoofed men and women who had attacked him earlier. They were digging through his bag, having dumped the gold in a pile beside them so they could get to his personal belongings.

One of them pulled a Roman coin from the pocket of his jeans and babbled excitedly in a language he didn't understand. A gift from Mila, the coin was worth more than all their lives put together, at least to him.

"Hey!" he roared.

The strange people jumped and backed away in fear.

"Put the fucking coin down, or I will end you all."

The man with the coin glanced at the ranger, who motioned for him to drop it. The man dropped the coin onto Finn's crumpled jeans, then made as if to squat and continue rummaging. Finn let out a long, low growl that made the top layer of sand vibrate and dance.

The naked people looked at one another, then ran across the sand in herd formation and dived into the water. They didn't come back up.

"You'll have to excuse the Kelpies." The girl drew Finn's attention. "They don't have much chance to socialize with humans, and they do love to collect baubles. They're worse than magpies, I swear."

She chuckled light-heartedly.

Finn moved closer to the fire and dropped into a cross-legged position, holding his cuffed hands out to the flames.

She eyed him critically. "You are a human, right? You're not like a troll or something with a concealment spell, are you?"

Finn almost said he was a dwarf, but he wanted to see where this was going, so instead, he just gave her a quizzical, raised eyebrow.

She chuckled again. "My name is Freya. I'm the dryad

of this island, and the Kelpies are my charges." She looked at him with a half-smile, but when he didn't respond, she frowned. "Look, I don't want to be a bitch here, but you gotta work with me, dude."

"Are all the ponies on the island Kelpies?" he asked, drawing another smile from Freya.

"Yeah, they are, though this particular breed must've been altered by someone a long time ago. They've been considerably dumbed down. Normal Kelpies are free to travel the seas and lakes at will. Did you know a Kelpie can swim across the Atlantic in less than three hours? That's some serious speed, man!" She clucked her tongue.

"Not these poor guys. They get more than ten miles out, and they start freaking. Not really sure what happened to them. I woke up one day, and there they were, crawling all over my island. I quickly realized that they needed serious taking care of, let me tell you."

"Don't they round up a bunch of the ponies each year and sell them?" Finn remembered that detail from Penny's thorough report on the island. "Doesn't sound like protecting them to me. Sounds like selling people for profit."

"It's not like that, man. These poor guys degrade as they get older. I can't figure out why, but when they hit around two or three years old, they get so dumb that they forget they're Kelpies and never change back to their human forms. At that point, they are, for all intents and purposes, just regular ponies. I started the pony-penning traditions so I could raise the capital to take care of the ones that needed it most. It's not a perfect system, but the ones that are sold live great lives. Chincoteague ponies are very much sought after. They get a good home, and the money helps the ones left behind."

"Why not just use the chests of gold to fund your operation? You could probably buy the whole island with what you have buried up there."

"It's complicated." She sighed. "We've got a pretty good thing going right now. The government funds most of the park, and the pony sale funds the extras. For now, it's the best move. Plus, the little guys just love to collect the stuff. They find stuff every other day, and we just throw it onto the pile."

She was silent for a bit, poking the fire and sending sparks into the air. Finn followed the trail and watched as one or two made it far enough to pass right through the stone.

He chuckled. The cave was just an illusion. It was a really good illusion, but still just an illusion.

"What so funny, fella?" she asked, smirking at him.

He shook his head. "Nothing. So, what are you planning on doing with me?"

She blew out a long breath. "Well, that's the thing, innit? I don't want to hurt you, but I'm afraid you've seen too much. I think we'll just meet in the middle and I'll turn you into a pony. You'll have a great life here. I'll take care of you, and you'll have plenty of friends. Don't worry, I'll dumb you down a bit, so you won't even remember being human. You'll see. It'll be great."

Finn chuckled again. "You know, I think I'll pass."

"Sorry, bub. You don't really have a say in the matter."

Finn slowly reached up and brushed his hair to the side, exposing the buzzed undercut. "Actually, I do."

The skin around his head where the undercut was began to glow with blue dwarven runes as he willed his "crown" to show. It was an inherited trait that only dwarves born into the royal family had, and it was recognizable across the galaxy.

Freya stood and backed away from him, almost tripping over the log she had been sitting on. "No, that's impossible. You're all dead. The dwarves have been gone for a thousand years."

"I'm new to town." He suppressed the crown and let his hair fall.

Freya's face went from terror to anger. "I will not be subject to another Dwarf King! That's the whole reason I left on this ship in the first place."

Finn held up his hands. "Calm down. Let's not do anything rash. We can work something out."

She screamed, and her features changed from a skinny tanned young woman without any distinguishing characteristics, into a willowy, beautiful woman with skin the color of mahogany that showed a light wood grain. Her brown hair turned a vibrant green like springtime leaves, and her teeth grew sharp and pointed.

"Freya, come on now. Let's talk this out."

She charged, her fingers twisting together to form into wooden spikes, and she drew her arms back as she ran to strike a deathblow.

Finn sighed.

He went from sitting to standing in one smooth movement. He pulled the chain of the cuffs apart like it was made of paper and reached into the front of his Speedo with one hand while he snatched her off the ground by the neck with the other.

A whispered word later and he had Fragar out and unfolded, glowing with a menacing dim purple nimbus.

Freya's eyes went wide as she stared at the axe that had seemingly come out of nowhere.

Finn set Fragar down, leaning the handle against a log before walking over to his pack and finding two of the four beers he had left and picking them up. He carried the beers and the dryad back over to the fire, and gently set Freya back on her log, where she sat frozen in fear. He took the log next to her and tossed her a beer.

She caught it, but only after fumbling it twice and almost dropping it into the fire.

Finn cracked his beer open and took a foamy sip. "Now, like I said, let's talk. I'll start. Hi, I'm Finn, king of the *Earth*." He laughed, but she just kept staring in fear. "That was a joke. Sorry."

He cleared his throat. "So, I have an idea that might help you."

She didn't say anything, just gave him the slightest of nods.

Finn took that as a good sign and started laying out his idea.

CHAPTER TWENTY-SEVEN

Victoria's condo took up the entire third floor of a three-story building that shared walls with a four-story building of apartments on one side and a two-story warehouse that had been converted into retail shops on the other. The building was in the Russian Hill neighborhood close to the famous Pier 39 shopping center.

She had them park the van in one of her parking spaces in the bottom floor garage, and they took an elevator that opened directly into her living room.

Carl had the team bring up a crate of various weapons and supplies, just in case, and they set up at the huge dining table that looked like it could seat twenty with plenty of elbow room.

Mila and Remmy were the last off the elevator, and Mila's jaw dropped when she saw the huge condo. It had to be two or three times the size of her place back in Denver, and they had recently doubled its size by buying the second condo on their floor and expanding into it.

The entire place was basically one room with modern-style wood and steel accents everywhere. An impressively done circular walled-off section filled the center of the space and housed the kitchen and a powder room, along with a wet bar on the living room side of the circle. Behind a door that was curved to disappear when closed was the laundry room.

To the left of the elevator, Mila found the dining table where the team pulled equipment out of their black crate

To the right of the elevator, the office, which took up a large section of the open floor plan, had a huge desk and multi-monitor computer system.

Along the front of the living room, a wall of windows looked out onto the street. Behind the elevator hid two bedrooms, both huge and equipped with their own master baths.

Victoria waved for Mila and Remmy to follow her. "Remmy was right, you smell like you were covered in blood and jumped into a ditch to wash off. Not that I'm any better."

"You have no idea how close that example was to the truth," Mila said, with a wry smile.

"I've been around long enough to know the smell of battle on someone." Victoria snorted, led them into the second bedroom, and slid open a closet door built into the wall so perfectly that Mila would have taken twenty minutes to find it. "There are towels and robes in here. I also have an assortment of underclothes you can change into. They are separated by size in these drawers here. If you want to wash what you have, the laundry is out in the main room behind the kitchen."

"Sweet!" Remmy opened one of the drawers and pulled

out a red lacy thong. "Why do you have extra clothes for guests?"

"Because I'm rich enough to."

Remmy nodded. "Makes sense to me. You want to go first, or do you want me to go?"

"Actually," Victoria interjected, "why don't you take this one, Remmy? Mila can come with me so we can talk while we get cleaned up."

"Works for me." Remmy walked into the bathroom, spinning the thong on her finger like a lasso.

"What an odd woman." Victoria laughed. "Come on, I have a robe you can use. I have to admit the leather you two are wearing is spotless, despite your face and under-shirt being covered in blood and grime."

"The leather is enchanted. Keeps itself clean and mended. Is my face really that dirty?" Mila swiped her face with a finger and felt a bit of grit flake off. "Ugh."

They walked into the main bedroom, which was laid out in a similar fashion to the guest room, only larger. Built-in closets and a vanity, along with a modern wooden king-sized bed and matching side tables, gave the large room a spartan but functional feel. The bathroom opened on the opposite side of the room as the one in the guest bedroom, but it still had the same large, doorless opening that revealed a completely white marble room, though only the sink and vanity could be seen from the bedroom.

Victoria opened a closet and pulled out two billowy white robes and tossed one to Mila. "I won't be long. There's a hamper in there for your underthings if you want to save them. Personally, I'm throwing all of this away." She plucked at her ruined blouse as she walked into the bath-room, leaving Mila to get undressed alone.

Mila walked to the bed and unzipped the black moto jacket. As she tossed the robe on the bed, she removed the jacket and examined it as she heard the shower in the bath-room behind her. She knew it was enchanted, but it still shocked her how clean it was. The leather didn't show so much as a scuff after the frantic fight, but still looked brand new.

Mila gave the jacket a thorough sniffing but couldn't smell anything but fresh leather. She sniffed her armpit just to be sure and was quickly convinced the enchanted leather was keeping itself clean.

She laid the jacket on the bed and marveled at how she actually did smell like a dumpster.

The pants came next. They were as clean as the moment she had put them on. Too bad she couldn't say the same for the rest of her clothes,

Her socks and underwear had not only been soaked with blood through her leggings during that first fight in the Market but had been put back on damp after her quick rinse in the alley with Remmy. She really didn't want to think about how gross they were now, so she pulled them off, along with the now-bloody white t-shirt and sports bra, crumbled them all up in a ball, and spiked them into the hamper.

As she slipped her arm into the robe, she felt the amazing quality of the fabric. By the time she had slid her other arm into the sleeve, she didn't know how she could ever be satisfied by another robe ever again. She felt like a cloud had come to life and hugged her all over.

As she sat on the bed to wait for Victoria to finish, Mila reached for her phone to call Finn but remembered that she had left it at home like an idiot.

"Mila," Victoria shouted to be heard over the water, "come in here so we can talk."

Mila rose and walked to the bathroom entrance. Inside, she spotted a plush bench against the far wall, past the vanity tucked in next to a large standalone tub. Opposite of the vanity and sink, the shower looked like a floor-to-ceiling frosted white glass box.

As she headed for the bench, Mila jumped when the top half of the shower door went from frosted white glass to clear in an instant to reveal Victoria's head and shoulders as she looked out into the bathroom and spotted Mila.

"Oh, there you are!" She went back to shampooing her hair. "We need to decide how best to deal with Azoth. I was able to contact every Valkyrie left out there, and had the Lones scatter to unknown locations, but I told the others to gather together, then head here. It'll take longer, but it will be much safer for them to travel together. I don't want one of Azoth's minions spotting them coming in one at a time; it might give away our location. Valkyries don't exactly travel quietly."

Mila was well aware of how visible they could be in the night sky. She was sure a lot of reports of ball lightning were more than likely people spotting a Valkyrie just going out for dinner.

"Why have the Lone Valkyries scatter? Doesn't that just leave them vulnerable in a new place? We should gather them in a safe location."

"They wouldn't do it. Coming together means they lose

their powers over time. You saw what it did to me when Azoth arrived with Sarah. Granted, I was already weak from the shackles, but you saw how debilitating that was. No one wants to put themselves through that on purpose."

Mila bit her lip, then frowned. That brought up something else that was bothering her. "About being drained when close to a Lone Valkyrie—"

"Why aren't you draining me right now?" Victoria rinsed the soap from her face before clearing the water from her eyes with a swipe of her hand. "I wondered when you would ask about that."

She chuckled. "That's another of those little details I hadn't told you yet. I didn't know how it was going to manifest, and I wanted you to have a strong understanding of what you could do before we addressed it."

"I'm not going to lie, Victoria. All this keeping things from me for my own good is not helping our friendship. I understand that in your mind, I have thousands of years to learn the intricacies of being a Valkyrie, but that's only true if I survive this battle with Azoth. I need information more than I need you to coddle me."

Victoria licked her lips, blinked water from her eyes, and regarded Mila through the glass. "I can appreciate that you feel like I might be cruel by keeping you in the dark about some things, but you have to understand that there are particular ways things have to be done when a new Valkyrie is born and brought into the fold. Frankly, our friendship is not high on my list of concerns; we don't have to be friends, we're sisters. And sometimes the elder sister has to do things that the younger sister doesn't like. Families are complicated like that. This is the way things are done when a child comes to us newly formed."

Mila snorted and shook her head in disbelief. "Victoria, we are *not* my family. Trust me, I know what a family is. I have a good one at home. Family is not a set of circumstances that forces you into a relationship. Family are the people you trust with your life, and who trust you in return. I don't give my trust freely, Victoria; you have to *earn* my trust. Keeping things from me because 'it's the way it's always been done' isn't good enough, not here in the midst of a war. I don't know if you've noticed, but this planet isn't like anywhere else in the universe. Things move fast here, and we don't have the luxury of space to maneuver or the time to do it in.

"From what I can gather, me being a Champion of a Hero, who I might add is a fucking Dwarf King, gives me an advantage over the rest of you, but I don't understand how or why. If I did, maybe I could leverage that advantage better and expand that advantage to the rest of the Valkyries."

Victoria sighed, then nodded as she shut off the shower. She opened the door, and the rest of the glass went clear to reveal a well-muscled body covered with hundreds of scars. She stepped out, took a towel from a heated wall rack, and turned to face Mila. "You're right, Mila. This is not a time for tradition or half-truths. You have a very difficult life ahead of you, one filled with fight after never-ending fight, and if you're lucky and can survive the battle, your best reward is to outlive everyone you love and watch them die of old age."

She waved a hand up and down her scarred body. "This

body is very old by Peabrain standards, and each of these scars is a memento from some asshole who thought they could control dark magic and instead went insane. They, almost to a man, died horrible all-consuming deaths, usually due to their own hubris. And do you want to know what the kicker is? It's that despite not one person mastering dark magic, they just keep trying, convinced that *they* will be the one to do it. So life turns into a never-ending battle, and even when there are decades between fights, they always come. But all of those battles are nothing compared to facing a Drude. A dark mage might be able to scar me with tainted magic, but I will not die from dark magic; I'll come back eventually. A Drude however, will eat your soul, and that will be it. No more Valkyrie.

"I wanted to spare you the reality of what you are. I wanted to know that at least one of us was truly happy for a lifetime before it all came crashing down. I wanted to spare you the horror of facing a Drude in all its power, so I kept you in the dark and feeling just helpless enough that you wouldn't go charging in headfirst," she snorted a sad laugh. "Turns out that you're not one to be deterred by things like certain death."

Mila smiled. "That's Finn's doing. I learned my determination from the best. Now, tell me what I need to know. We have a lot to do before we're done, and being informed is just as important as being prepared."

Victoria nodded, dried herself off, and turned to the mirror over the sink. "May as well hop in the shower. This might take a little time."

Mila smiled and walked over to the towel rack as she untied the robe.

"The first thing you need to know is that newborn Valkyries have the ability to adapt to the situation they find themselves in by absorbing the traits and abilities of those around them. This sounds weird, but if you think of Valkyries as antibodies to the evil in the universe, then it makes a little more sense. A new threat means a new type of antibody to fight it. By augmenting your natural abilities with those of the people around you, you can become something unique to fight off an otherwise unstoppable enemy."

Mila pulled her robe off and hung it on a wall hook. "So, I'm gaining abilities from Finn, Penny, and Danica?"

"More than likely, although your ability to channel celestial magic is still going to be your defining trait."

Mila narrowed her eyes and looked at Victoria in the mirror she faced. "Can you see in the dark?"

Victoria shrugged. "Better than most if I enhance my vision with magic."

"Interesting." Mila turned her back to Victoria and opened the shower door.

"What is that?" Victoria asked, her voice tight.

"What?" Mila looked over her shoulder and realized Victoria had spotted the tattoo Finn had created for her at the small of her back. "Oh, Finn gave it to me. He said it's the mark of a Shield Maiden. I guess they're, like, the most badass of the king's guards."

"I know who the Shield Maidens are, but how do you have it?" Victoria turned and bent close to examine it.

"Finn gave it to me."

"Yes, but this is an empowered mark. It's not just a symbol; you're marked as an actual Shield Maiden. If you somehow went to the Dwarven Palace, they would give you complete access because you can't fake this mark. Only the Emperor can give this mark out."

"Well, I don't think Finn is one to always follow the rules," Mila half-joked.

Victoria growled in frustration. "No, you don't understand. I'm not saying no one but the Emperor is *allowed* to give out this mark, I'm saying that no one but the Emperor *can* give out this mark. Even if Finn is his son, he shouldn't be able to give you this mark...unless he's become a Dwarf King in his own right."

"Well, he does always joke that he's the Dwarf King of Earth. You know, since he's the only dwarf on the planet."

"He might not be joking."

"What does that mean?" Mila asked, more curious than concerned.

"Well, if you're absorbing abilities and powers from Finn, and the universe somehow recognizes him as an actual Dwarf King... I have no idea. That's not something that's ever happened before. By the end of this, you might not be a Valkyrie."

"Well, then." Mila stepped into the shower and turned it on. "You better explain what you can while I'm still Valkyrie enough to benefit from it."

Victoria shook her head in wonder. "Well, I guess it won't hurt at this point. Do you know what entropy is?"

"This sounds fun," Mila said sarcastically.

CHAPTER TWENTY-EIGHT

Mila grabbed a beer and headed up a set of stairs hidden behind a wall panel that led up to the roof, which had been converted into a giant wooden patio. Lights strung across the entire roof blinked on as the sun began to set and cast a warm glow across the deck.

Benches and stone fire pits had been set in the corners of the patio, with a full bar that had been shuttered for storage. In the center of the patio, several very nice wicker and cloth club-style chairs sat around a large coffee table that had a gas fire pit in the middle.

From this side of the hill, Mila had an unobstructed view of the bay in front of her, the Golden Gate Bridge to her left and Oakland to her right. The sky had begun to turn a burnt orange, with pink and purple highlights reflecting off the water.

Mila took a deep breath and zipped up the moto jacket as the breeze picked up and cut through the V-neck black t-shirt she had gotten from the guest closet, along with a full set of underclothes.

As she took a seat in one of the club chairs, she twisted the top off the beer and looked out over the bay as the light began to fade.

"Would you look at that view." Carl's head popped up over the edge of the building from the alley side of the roof.

"Hey, Carl! What the hell are you doing, man?" Mila asked, beer bottle frozen halfway to her mouth.

He glanced over in surprise. "Oh, hey, Mila. I didn't see you there. I'm just making sure we have good access to the fire escapes if we need them."

He climbed up onto the roof patio and headed her way to take a seat in one of the chairs. "I rang Preston while you were in the shower. He's sending a couple of teams. They should be here in just over an hour. At about the same time, Victoria's expecting the other Valkyries to arrive. The plan is pretty simple; the G.A.E.L. teams will breach the building and fill the place with gravity grenades. Really discombobulate the shit out of 'em before the Valkyries head in. We bring up the rear and provide what support we can. Plan is for us to take care of the minions while you guys hit the big boys. With us taking shots of opportunities."

Mila bit her lip and looked out over the bay. "It's not enough. We need more muscle. Can I borrow your phone? I left mine at home."

"Isn't that a phone in your hand?"

Mila lifted the phone and shook her head. "This here is a Valkyrie comm device," she joked. "Actually, that's not too far off. This phone only works to call other phones on the list. Basically, it's secure communication for the Valkyries."

Carl pulled a phone from a hip pouch he had attached as part of his tactical gear. "No long distance." He laughed at her surprised face. "Just kidding. Preston pays for it, so you can call the Moon for all I care. I assume you're calling your boyfriend in?"

Mila nodded. "And my dragon friend. Hopefully, she found what she was looking for. If I know her, she found a way to turn Azoth into a whiny little bitch."

"That would be a nice change of pace." Carl smirked. "I'll give you a little privacy. I need to check the escape on the other side anyway."

He left her, headed to the street side of the building, climbed over the short wall, and disappeared down a ladder that was out of sight.

Mila opened the phone, punched in Finn's number, and hit send. She waited while it rang twice and picked up.

"Finn?" she asked, more excited than she should have been.

"How the fuck does this thing work?" she heard him grumble, then her own voice in the background. "It's recording, just go." Then Finn came back louder than the first time as he put the phone to his ear. "This is Finn. Leave a message or a text. No, fuck that, leave a message."

Mila laughed and hit the end button. She remembered when he had recorded that. It was odd to hear since he usually picked up on the first ring. He must be out of range.

She dialed Penny's number, hoping the little dragon had taken her phone with her.

Penny picked up on the first ring. "Chi?"

"Penny, it's Mila."

"Shi shir chi?"

Mila furrowed her brow. "Man, it is really hard trying to understand you in audio only. Did you just ask if I've ever had a daiquiri? Like, a strawberry daiquiri?"

There was a series of angry shouts from Penny and a man and a woman in the room with her.

"Penny, hang on. I'm going to call you back." Mila hung up and dialed Penny again, but this time connected the call through video.

Penny answered right away. All Mila could see was Penny's belly as she backed away from the camera after answering. The angle of the phone made it look like she was about six inches tall and standing on a long wooden table that was covered in dark metal pieces. It looked like it could be one of those sculpture puzzles.

Penny finally backed up so her whole body was in view. "Chi?"

"Yes, much better. Where are you?" Mila squinted at the screen in hopes of making out what was on the table.

"Chi shee shiri shir," Penny waved her arm toward the end of the table where a woman about Mila's age with a vibrant blue pixie cut and a shoulder exposed out of a wide-necked knit shirt leaned into the frame.

The woman waved, a smile on her face. "Hi, you must be this Mila we've heard so much about. I'm Rebecca Breck, and this is my husband Lance."

She held up her arm, and a pudgy man with curly blond hair leaned into frame. Rebecca kissed him on the cheek as he waved.

"Hello, Mila. Can't wait to meet you." He moved out of the frame.

"Oh, uh…" Mila had no clue who those people were.

Rebecca snorted. "He's just messing with you, although we would like to meet you and Finn at some point."

"I mean, any friend of Penny's is a friend of mine. Just one quick question. Who *are* you guys?"

For the next five minutes, Penny related her journey since that morning, from finding the name Breck, a supposed chronicler and artificer, and ending with going to the Louisiana bayou and meeting Rebecca, Lance, and Grimmly.

"Hold up, Penny. You're telling me that this Gregory not only told Missy she was full of shit but then built a device that could kill a Drude? And that's it on the table?" Mila sat up straight.

"Shir shee," Penny corrected.

"Sorry, he designed it. But that's it? You guys built it?"

"Well, we're still building it. We have a couple of pieces left to make, then we need to put it together," Rebecca explained.

Mila's heart was starting to beat quicker with excitement. "How does it work?"

Penny let Rebecca do the explaining since she had the plans in front of her. "Theoretically, if it's charged up and touches a Drude, it will release its pent-up energy to flood into the Drude, temporarily pulling it fully into the corporeal world. Then it's just a matter of killing it like you would anything else."

Mila narrowed her eyes. "Theoretically?"

Rebecca gave a tight-lipped smile and shrugged. "Yeah. He never built one, and even if he had, he couldn't test it. It takes celestial magic to work. Basically, his idea is that since celestial and infernal magic cancel one another out, and a Drude keeps it's magic stored in a separate reality by sort of straddling the line between realities, the best way to bring the Drude completely into the corporeal world is to flood it with celestial magic. The magics would cancel each other out and basically burn out everything the Drude has. Since it uses it's magic to keep the connection between realities open, that would shut down, leaving just the body. But it would only last as long as it took for it to regain even a tiny bit of magic."

"It's like what happens to Valkyries and Lone Valkyries when they get too close. Our magic cancels out..." Mila stared off into the distance, an idea forming, but too outlandish to be true. "Could a Valkyrie be infected with infernal magic that doesn't come from a Drude? Like just out in the wild? No, that wouldn't make sense. It's not the Drude that the magic reacts to, but the opposite magic. What if it's the part of us that we use to go to Elsewhere..." She was talking to herself, but the others were still listening, and Mila jumped when Rebecca answered her.

"That's an interesting idea. Actually, Gregory had a theory about that," she said, flipping through an old book on the table in front of her. "Here it is. He believed that 'by using the Reaper it introduced a taint in the Valkyrie's soul.'" She looked up at the camera, a slightly confused look on her face. "I don't know what the Reaper is, but that sounds like what you're talking about."

Mila nodded, the pieces starting to fall into place in her mind, but she felt like there was a big piece that went right in the middle that she just couldn't see. And lots of questions that needed answering first, like why did the draining effect stop happening to her? What had changed between the first time she and Victoria had met and this time?

She grimaced. It would have to be a question for later.

"How long until you will be finished with the device?"

Penny and Rebecca spoke quietly for a second then Penny turned back to the camera. "Chi squee?"

Mila sighed. "Three hours is too long. We have an opportunity to corner Azoth and his entire organization in an hour. We're gathering as many fighters as we can. Preston's even sending two more of his teams to support us. It's the best opportunity we're going to have, but there are only seven Valkyries left who can fight. The other eight —seven now—are Lone Valkyries. I'm afraid it won't be enough. But the teams all get here in about an hour, and if we wait too long, he'll be in the wind again, if he's not already."

Rebecca and Penny had another quiet discussion, and this time Lance joined in. Eventually, Rebecca came back to Mila. "We think we can get it done in an hour, but Penny's going to be spent. I can teleport her to your location to save her the long flight, but we will need to push to get done that fast. And remember, this thing hasn't ever been tested. It might work perfectly, or it might cause a huge explosion when the magics interact on that kind of level. It will also need to be charged, which if I'm reading this right is a lot of magic. Like, 'this has to be a mistake' a lot."

"Okay, I'll bring it up to Victoria and see what she thinks, but I would really appreciate it as an option."

"You got it. We'll make it happen."

"Shiri shee chi?"

"I called him, but it went to voicemail. I'm going to try again after I hang up." Mila gave them the address of Victoria's condo and made her goodbyes, with a promise to come and meet Rebecca and Lance soon.

After hanging up, she redialed Finn and hit send.

The voice mail picked up again, and she snorted at the message again, then she heard the beep.

"Hey, Manther, it's Darlin'." She chuckled before continuing, "So, we have a bit of a situation going on. I already let Penny know, and she's going to be here in an hour or so. We have Azoth's location, along with his entire little army, but I feel like we could really use a dwarf in the mix. We're staging at Victoria's San Francisco condo." She gave him the address. "If you can, come. If not, I'll be just fine. We're going in all guns blazing. Oh, if you do make it and kill twenty bad guys, I'll buy you a pair of enchanted ass-less chaps as a reward; Remmy knows a guy. Just wanted to let you know there would be prizes for participation." Mila sighed, silent for a second. "I love you, babe. I hope you're having a good time at the beach, and I'm sure it's very pretty there, but I have to say the view from this roof deck is amazing." She looked out over the bay as the last of the sun's light faded and the millions of city lights replaced it.

A moving spot of light in the sky caught her attention. When she focused on it, she immediately recognized the lightning ball effect that the Valkyries used to travel fast. After watching the streaking ball for a second, she could tell it was headed her way.

"Hey, babe, it looks like the other Valkyries are arriving." The lightning ball started to fall towards her. "Get here quick if you can. But don't feel bad if you can't. I just know how much you like a fight." She crossed her arms and looked down, putting the phone close to her mouth. "I love you. I know I already said that, but fuck you, I'll say it as much as I want. Okay. See you here, or see you at home."

She looked back up and the lightning ball was practically on top of her, coming in at breakneck speed. Her eyes went wide when she saw that at the center of the crackling ball was Missy, a long silver sword in one hand, a black-spiked gauntlet on the other, and a maniacal grin on her face.

"Oh, fuck!" Mila dropped the phone and threw her arms up to protect herself.

CHAPTER TWENTY-NINE

Mila created a shield and flooded her body with power just as Missy slammed her gauntlet into the golden barrier.

Light flashed from the impact and blew Mila off her feet. She tumbled across the roof, to slam into one of the wicker chairs. It slid across the deck, the side crumpled in.

Mila reached behind her, grabbed Gram with her right hand and the Ivar with her left, and yanked both weapons out at the same time. She activated her mythril armor and Gram with two whispered words. She bounced to her feet before the sword reached full extension, but Missy swung the silver longsword in a side arc that would take Mila's head off.

Her heightened reflexes and muscle got Gram up just in time. The two swords clanged together to send a shower of sparks to the floor as Missy's blade slid down the length of Gram.

Mila shot the Ivar from her hip, the magical bolt racing out at point-blank range, but Missy had a shield up to block it. The raw magic slammed into the semi-invisible barrier and exploded, sending both women flying apart.

Mila crashed into a glass table and chairs, a hastily erected shield keeping her from being hurt too badly as the glass shattered, and the chairs flew into the wall with a loud metallic clatter.

Mila landed badly and found herself draped over a now half-crumpled chair. Mila took a second to get to her feet, a second too long.

A silver sword jabbed into Mila's stomach, doubled her over, and drove her into the ruined table. She twisted and fell over the frame, then through the empty opening where the glass had been to get tangled up with the table legs.

Her ribs screamed in pain where the point of the sword had jabbed them. Her mythril was enough to stop the blade, but it had still hurt like a motherfucker. It seemed that Missy wasn't as willing to use her portion of infernal magic as Yaminah had been, or it was so small a portion that she couldn't. That was fine with Mila; she didn't want to have to worry about her mythril being cut thorough, but that was a hell of a way to test Missy's abilities.

Missy raised her sword over her head to chop down at Mila's legs, but Mila reached down with the Ivar and touched a finger to the ground. At the speed of thought, she sent a burst of magic and a force of will to shape it within the deck boards.

As Missy's sword came down in an overhand chop, the deck boards below her warped and cracked, then exploded upward into a million high-speed splinters.

Missy screamed in pain as she flew ten feet into the air, several dozen long splinters stuck in her legs and arms.

Not wanting to waste an opportunity, Mila aimed the Ivar and hit the screaming Valkyrie in the chest with a bolt of magic. A flashing boom sent Missy tumbling end over end in an arc that ended with her slamming to the deck chest-first. Her head bounced once before she groaned and folded into a fetal position.

Mila pulled herself out of the remains of the table and aimed the Ivar at the blue-haired girl.

The groans slowly turned to laughter as Missy climbed to her feet. The right shoulder of her long sleeve black t-shirt had been shredded and there was a gaping wound four inches around, dripping blood rapidly.

"I didn't want to have to do this, but you're just a little too full of surprises." Missy's eyes narrowed and her teeth clenched.

The blood slowed, then stopped, and black steam began to rise from the wound as it closed within the span of a few seconds.

Missy rolled her shoulder and grinned, locking eyes with Mila.

Mila took aim with the Ivar as Missy charged. As Mila pulled the trigger, the bolt shot out of the pistol at incredible speed toward Missy's chest.

At the last second, Missy spun to her left, dodged the projectile, and raced towards Mila, her speed augmented to unbelievable levels. The distance shrank faster than Mila could comprehend.

A golden wing of light blocked Mila's view as Victoria stepped between them to block Missy's charge.

The two Valkyries slammed into one another, their shields out and crackling with golden light.

Victoria was shoved back several feet, her sneakers leaving black marks across the boards.

She stopped only a foot or two in front of Mila, her wings spread wide as she stood tall. The golden-orange color of the insubstantial wings roiled like molten iron. Mila could see now that the wings were not actually attached to Victoria's back, If she looked past the wings, she could see that they were translucent.

Mila scooted back and to the side to give Victoria room to move, and so that she would have a sightline on Missy.

The two eldest Valkyries stood a dozen feet apart, their faces hard as they stared into one another's eyes. Victoria's weapon wasn't what Mila would have expected the tall, elegant woman to carry. She had expected a rapier or saber, but in her hands she held a five-foot-long falchion.

The blade of the huge weapon didn't have a pointed tip like a traditional sword but rather had a flat end. The blade tapered from four inches wide at the end to about two inches where the long leather-wrapped handle started. It had no cross-guard or pommel. A falchion was not a finesse weapon. It was not a fast weapon. It wasn't even a pretty weapon. A falchion was the weapon of a savage fighter who screamed curses into the faces of the gods. It was the weapon of a maniac.

Finn would love one.

"Why?" Victoria shook with rage. "Why are you doing this? Betraying your sisters to that…thing?"

A look of shame flashed across Missy's face before it hardened again. "I'm done with this fucking piece-of-shit vessel! It was supposed to be only a few hundred years, then we would go home, but that fucking Huldu couldn't be bothered to do his cursed job and gets us stuck out in the ass-end of the universe. Hundreds of years turned to thousands, and we're still here, Victoria. Unless I do something, we were going to be here forever. I had a mission, and now I can complete it. It cost lives, but this is war, sister. People die all the time. It was an acceptable cost."

"So that's it? You'd sell your sisters into eternal death just so you can get home? You don't think we want to go home too? Are we not worth the same, you and I?"

Missy clenched her teeth in anger as she glared daggers at Victoria. "You're the one who sold us out, Victoria. Look at you! You don't want to leave. You have your money and your power, and you can act like a god among men here. But I remember what it was like for you back home; always looked over for promotion, always reprimanded for your viciousness. You were an animal, Victoria. You might play the part of a high society bitch here, but I've seen the things you've done in the name of victory.

"We got stuck here, and you saw an opportunity to start over. To make yourself into something more than you ever could be out there. You wanted to stay. You've always been willing to sacrifice the mission for your own gain.

"Well, I wasn't. I had a life out there. I had a home and a wife who loved me. I lost all that, and you were more than happy to let me suffer for your gains."

Tears ran down Missy's cheeks, but her face was still a mask of fury.

"That's not what happened, Missy," Victoria said as the fire in her voice dimmed to be replaced by confusion. "I wasn't keeping you here. I didn't sacrifice your life out there for my own gain; I made the best of the situation we were in. The taint in you is corrupting your emotions, Missy. Don't you remember us trying to get home? We spent a thousand years combing through every cargo hold and private residence trying to find any way home we could."

Missy barked a laugh. "A thousand years? What is that to us? You might as well have looked for ten minutes."

"Why would you let him take you?" Mila asked.

Something about all of this didn't make sense.

The two Valkyries seemed to have forgotten she was there.

"You made a deal with Azoth," Mila continued, determined to understand. "I'm guessing that if you fed him some of your sisters so he could regain his power, he promised to take you away from *Earth*, but what did he get in return? And how did you know he was going to awaken? Unless…"

"What are you talking about?" Victoria asked, frustrated that Mila was interfering, but Mila didn't give a fuck. There was a missing puzzle piece she needed to find.

"She awoke five years ago." Mila looked at Missy "Yeah, we know you're not fifteen. So she wakes up and her parents die in a crash, then nothing until she shows up claiming the last five years never happened. You knew the Drude wasn't dead. You also knew he could potentially take you home. You woke him up, didn't you? That's what you were doing for those five years. You were waking that creature up and putting your plan into motion."

"I needed to do my research," Missy said, a smile growing on her face. "You are a clever girl, aren't you? I knew you were going to be a problem the second I heard about you.

"You're right, I watched and learned, mostly about where and how my sisters were protecting themselves. After all, I needed a quick way in and out if I was going to be taking Valkyries by surprise. How else would I know to come here to find you?"

Mila saw from the corner of her eye Carl and Tina climb over the wall behind Missy to take defensible positions.

"But why did you let him take you? I understand that you have to be a thrall of his to be taken off-planet, but why now? Why so early? Why not when you're ready to leave?" Mila asked. Then her face brightened. "He tricked you. He said he was ready to go, but once he took you, he controlled you. Now you're just his puppet."

Missy started laughing. "If you only knew the truth. I know what I'm doing, child."

She tossed a flat stone pulled from the waistband of her skirt to the deck.

"No!" Victoria screamed, but it was too late.

The stone hit the floor and flashed with black energy. A circle of black power rushed out in all directions. When the circle hit a ward, there was a flash of gold, but it quickly died under the wave of infernal magic.

Within seconds, the entire building had been stripped of its wards.

Twenty void portals ripped open across the rooftop and thralls, and Rougarou poured out by the dozens.

CHAPTER THIRTY

Spells and silenced rifle fire lit up the night, as the G.A.E.L. team opened fire on the minions. Thralls and Rougarou went down fast, but for every one killed, two more came out of a portal.

Missy rushed towards Victoria, her own golden wings unfurling the moment sword and falchion crashed together to ring out over the sounds of battle all around them.

At the first strike between the two Valkyries, Mila noticed the sky darkened with storm clouds that formed out of nothing. At the second clash, lightning streaked through the clouds, making them glow purple and angry. Another clash and more lightning flashed as thunder rolled across the city.

Mila jumped back as a Rougarou charged and took a swipe at her. She landed on her back foot, then sprang forward to take the wolfman's head in a single strike. A pack of four thralls charged her and she danced to the side, then cut two down with Gram and sent a bolt from the Ivar to blow a large hole through the other two.

On deciding the overflowing minions were the larger threat, Mila charged into the fray, Gram singing through the air to slice the enemy into bloody chunks.

After chopping down three thralls, Mila dropped to one knee as a Rougarou slashed thorough the empty air where her head had just been. Before she could react, the giant beast doubled over, howling in pain as something sliced its belly wide open. The Rougarou fell to the deck, still twitching as Remmy materialized in front of it, her daggers covered in blood.

"Heya, boss." She saluted, then sucked in a deep breath and disappeared.

Mila smiled. That little goblin lived for this stuff.

Mila shot off another bolt that ripped through a bunched-up group of thralls that tried to flank Howard and Jenny. Jenny nodded thanks, then threw a gravity grenade to the far corner of the roof where three of the portals stood open to dump enemies at an alarming rate. With a blue flash, two dozen thralls and Rougarou were sucked into the epicenter where their bodies crushed each other. Then the field reversed, and bodies flew in all directions. Most slammed into the wall next to them, but a few were tossed twenty feet into air only to smack into the deck.

As the crowd thinned around her, Mila took aim at Missy. She started to pull the trigger, but a chill ran over her arms. She spun around and threw her shield up just in time to intercept a black dagger. The shield screamed and sparked as the blade slowly plunged into the flashing gold barrier, only to be stopped by the dagger's own hilt.

Mila heard a sizzle from her pant leg and moved it to the side to avoid more of the dripping black magic from the dagger's tip. She looked up to see the crazed face of Yaminah.

"Dammit, woman!" Mila screamed up at the vicious woman. "These are new pants!"

She slammed her fist to the deck and willed the floor beneath Yaminah to burst into a pillar of flame. The mage danced back to dodge most of the spell but left her blade stuck in Mila's shield, smacking at her pants to put out a small fire.

Mila dropped the shield, avoided the falling dagger, and let it thunk to the deck. With a sharp kick to the flat of the blade, she sent it skittering across the boards and under a built-in bench.

The almost continual lightning above them that was somehow a reaction to the Valkyries' fighting caused a bit of a strobe effect. When Yaminah lifted her hand and shot three sets of three diamond-shaped missiles at her, Mila could see the whole thing in stop-motion.

It seemed to be a weak attack, considering how easy it was to see coming. Mila put up her shield and took the nine missiles against it, each exploding and leaving a purple cloud behind.

But Yaminah had used the missiles as a diversion and circled around Mila's shield. Mila realized her mistake as soon as a dagger sliced across her back, cutting through the leather, t-shirt, and mythril with ease.

Mila arched her back and gasped as the infernal

magical coating of the blade burned its way into her muscle. She spun to protect herself from another attack, but Yaminah wasn't there anymore, and another slash, this one at her mid-back, burned into her.

Mila sent a little healing to the two cuts and felt her stores of magic dip considerably, but the burning stopped, and she felt the wounds close. She needed to avoid healing if she was going to last the rest of the battle.

She started to pivot again, just like last time, then reversed the move and launched herself forward, her shield leading. Just as she'd thought, Yaminah had tried the same move again, but this time Mila caught her and slammed into the surprised woman like a charging bull.

Mila pumped her legs like a front linesman and drove the off-balance woman towards the edge of the building. Mila knew a three-story fall wouldn't be enough to kill someone like Yaminah, but it should be enough to get her out of the fight long enough to clear out the rest of the minions.

When she saw what Mila planned, Yaminah put her back to the shield. The moment they were close enough, she planted her feet on the short wall at the edge of the roof and kicked off to slide up the shield and flip over Mila's head.

Half expecting something ridiculous from the woman, Mila slashed backward with Gram. The sword slammed into Yaminah's dagger, and the golden blade slid down the dagger to jam into the crossguard.

"Fucking hell, it's like I'm fighting Finn or something!" Mila shouted in frustration. "Always with the counter-move! I fucking hate it!"

"Do better, then!" Yaminah jumped back and flung a spell at Mila's face.

Mila dropped to her knees as a green ball of acid shot over her head. Then she pivoted to the side but kept her shield arm where it was.

In a move that shocked both Mila and Yaminah, the acid splashed onto the spherical interior of Mila's shield, making it glow and crackle as it resisted the acid spray. The watery caustic fluid shot down the front and out the bottom of the curved surface of the shield's interior, to splash back at Yaminah's booted feet.

The other woman danced backward but got a bit of the magical fluid on the tip of her boot. The leather quickly split and began to smoke.

Mila saw the battle in full view from the edge of the roof. Eighty percent of the minions had gone down, and the rest were desperately fighting a losing battle with Carl and his team. Mila's eyes widened when she got her first glimpse of Nick in the fight. How she had missed the enormous brown bear crushing thralls and Rougarou alike she had no idea, but the addition of Remmy riding on his back like some Russian cavalry unit from hell, made her really glad she had.

Someone had given the goblin a rifle and she made the most of it, whooping and hollering as she pumped rounds into a charging eight-foot-tall wolfman. It was a hell of a thing to see, and she knew it would be an image that stuck with her for the rest of her life.

The hairs on Mila's arms stood on end, and she glanced up to see that the lightning was almost continuous at this point. Each time the two elder Valkyries struck their blades together, another flash of electricity ripped through the sky. Mila felt like she could just reach up and grab it.

Her scalp tingled at the idea.

Yaminah was suddenly in her face. Mila, distracted by the pull of the storm, hadn't noticed her charge, and she was almost too late to dodge a slash at her throat.

As she leaned back, the short wall at the roof's edge digging into the small of her back, Mila was able to get just out of reach. She kicked out, but Yaminah caught her foot, and to Mila's horror, used its momentum to lift her up and over the wall.

Mila dropped her weapons and scrambled to catch hold of the edge of the roof as her body slammed into the outside wall and her feet dangled three stories up.

Above her, she saw the disappointed face of Yaminah looking down at her, the black dagger in her hand, poised over Mila's fingers.

"I thought you were better than that." The hard woman tossed her long single braid over her shoulder.

Mila heard the words, but she couldn't focus on Yaminah since the lightning mesmerized her. She felt as if the storm was alive and calling to her. It wanted her to intercede for it. It desperately wanted to connect the heavens and the Earth.

"I hoped you were better than that." Yaminah sounded sorrowful as she brought the knife down to chop Mila's fingers off and drop her from the roof.

Mila didn't feel fear, she felt sorrow—sorrow for those that would stand against her. Sorrow that she couldn't save everyone. Sorrow for Yaminah and the bad life choices that had led her to her destruction.

Something at the base of Mila's skull snapped open and a flood of power rushed into her. Suddenly the lightning wasn't all the way up in the clouds out of her reach, it lay in her hand. She just needed to command it.

She did.

A white spear of pure energy lanced down from the clouds, crackled its way joyously to the Earth, and enveloped Yaminah, outlining her body in blinding white light as it crashed down to drive its power into the building.

The bolt retreated as fast as it had come and thunder followed, a physically painful sound that tore at Mila's senses, making her ears ring and her vision blur.

The wall she hung onto felt warm under her fingers.

With a little effort, Mila pulled herself over the wall to take in the aftermath of what she had done. The deck boards for ten feet in every direction of the lightning strike had been turned to smoke. A dozen thralls scattered across the charred wood bits had obviously been caught in the strike.

Luckily, her weapons were made of sturdier stuff than the deck and had survived without a scratch. She bent down to retrieve Gram and the Ivar and brushed a few wood chips from the pistol's handle.

When she looked up, Mila realized everyone on the roof was staring at her. Even Missy and Victoria, although their expressions were far different. Victoria had a look of awe, and Missy had a look of disgusted horror.

The remaining two dozen thralls had been knocked down by the blast but quickly scrambled to their feet and charged at Carl's team, which opened fire once again. The only two Rougarou left crouched on the floor and held their sensitive ears. Nick and Remmy moved to make quick work of them.

"Well, that was something." Mila scratched her scalp, then walked toward them with slightly drunken steps.

CHAPTER THIRTY-ONE

"A re you done?" Mila called to Missy, nearly tripping on a dead thrall.

Missy sneered. "I don't think you understand what's at stake here, child. This is not something I can just walk away from, not anymore."

"I'll take that as a no," Mila said, her eyes narrowing as she called down a second lightning strike, blasting the spot where Missy stood.

Blinding light and a terrible ripping thunder blasted boards to splinters.

The thing at the back of Mila's skull cracked open further, and more power flooded into her.

She called down another bolt, slamming it into the same spot again. This one was twice the size of the first two.

The windows of the surrounding buildings exploded, showering glass to the streets for a block in every direction.

Like a dam giving way, the thing in her skull was overrun, all blockage washed away in a torrent of celestial magic.

Mila had no clue what was happening, but she knew whatever it was, it wasn't supposed to happen like this. She felt like that guy who levels up in a video game, skipping ahead but unprepared for the next enemies because he doesn't have the right equipment.

The light of the second strike faded, revealing Missy standing tall, her silver longsword planted in the deck and a glowing golden shield surrounding her.

"You shouldn't be able to do that, child," the blue-haired woman said smugly.

"Fuck you?"

"No thanks, but you did show me yours; perhaps it's time I show you mine." She smirked, stabbing her sword into the wood and letting go, using the deck as a holder.

Missy's brow furrowed with heated concentration. Her body began to glow with golden light. It pulsed and grew in intensity, becoming brightest at the center of her chest. Then a black speck appeared in the swirling golden light, and sweat sprang up out her brow.

Small, thin root-like structures started to spread from the dark spot. Wherever the roots reached, the light dimmed but also took on a violet color. Missy's expression changed from concentration to pain, but she continued to force the merger of powers.

Mila was having a difficult time understanding what was happening. The infernal magic should be canceling out the celestial; it didn't make any sense. Unless the magics could mix if they came from the same host?

In the end, it didn't matter. It was happening before her eyes.

The spot had gone from coin- to basketball-sized and was growing quickly. Missy buried her face in her hands and began to scream.

Mila and Victoria locked gazes, and the elder nodded.

Flooding her body with power, Mila felt herself become stronger than ever. When she launched herself forward, she was moving at a speed she had only seen Victoria and Missy achieve. In three quick strides, she had crossed the destroyed deck and was swinging Gram at Missy's bowed head, while Victoria swung her huge falchion at her side.

Missy reached her gauntleted hand out faster than Mila could follow and a black wall formed, making Victoria's heavy sword rebound, ringing in her hands. Gram did not encounter a black wall; it hit a golden shield, biting into the barrier but not splitting it by any means.

The entire time they attacked, she had never stopped screaming, and now that scream grew in intensity. She threw her head back, eyes closed and fists clenched at her sides.

Mila and Victoria stepped back, watching in horror as Missy's golden wings began to drip ink-black smoke from their feather tips. In seconds, the black color at the tips had crawled halfway up each of the flight feathers, leaving the bottom half of each wing covered in a translucent dripping black substance.

Missy's scream cut off and she lowered her head slowly, a smile on her face. "I've been waiting to do that for five years." She moved her head sharply to the side, cracking her neck. "It was better than I thought."

Mila recoiled when Missy finally opened her eyes. Her pupils had been replaced with a deep void that looked like the inside of Azoth's hood, but where Azoth contained his void, Missy's eyes seemed to be leaking. A thin line of turbulent, sticky black smoke spilled out, rolling up her forehead to create a kind of smoky crown.

"You didn't take his infernal magic," Mila said in horror. "You took a part of his soul."

"Now you begin to understand."

The roof had gone quiet. Missy looked around at the carnage and the five members of the G.A.E.L. team pointing spell-prepped hands or wands and weapons alike. Remmy sucked in a breath and vanished, while Veronica tightened her grip on her massive weapon.

"Seems you have me at a disadvantage." Missy chuckled, locking eyes with Mila. "Perhaps it's time I go."

"I'm not letting you out of my sight," Mila said, raising Gram in a defensive position.

"I can live with that," Missy remarked before taking a step back, stomping her foot, and sending out a shock wave that blasted all of Carl's people but Nick onto their asses. Nick, however, was shoved back a good ten feet, the fur on his face and front legs flattening.

Missy then launched herself at Victoria, swiping her sword, while at the same time igniting it with black infernal fire. Victoria threw up a shield and ducked, and yelped in fear when the enhanced sword sliced through the shield with barely any resistance and missed her head by less than an inch.

Mila didn't hesitate, stabbing out with Gram. She aimed for Missy's back, but a black shield formed just as the point was about to hit, and it skipped off. She followed the sword strike with a blast from the Ivar, but Missy simply ducked under it and swung her gauntlet in a backhand swing that caught Mila on the shoulder, knocking her to the deck.

Victoria stood from her crouch, swinging the falchion in an uppercut that caught the edge of Missy's hastily erected golden shield and lopped one of her blue pigtails off.

"You fucking bitch!" Missy screamed, her gauntlet going to her head to feel the spiky remains of the tail as three feet of blue hair spilled across the ground.

In a rage, Missy's flaming longsword stabbed at Victoria, who was still stretched at an odd angle after her upward swing. She was able to throw up a shield, which deflected the strike at first, but the black flames quickly ate through the shield and the sword pierced Victoria's jeans to stab deeply into her thigh.

Victoria screamed as the black flames burned her from the inside. She fell off the sword and onto the deck, grasping her wound, continuing to scream as black flames licked out of the gash and caught her jeans on fire.

Mila made a move to help, but a thick blast of infernal mist roiled toward her from Missy's gauntlet, forcing her to take cover behind a shield. Even with her increased power, the mist was eating through her shield at a shocking rate.

Mila touched the floor and willed a line of flame from the front of her shield and out ten feet. Magic drained from her and the deck in front of her exploded with white-hot flames, cutting off the caustic mist, but Mila lost sight of Missy in the confusion. She looked left and saw a void portal beside her. She hadn't noticed she had gotten that close to one, but when she looked right, she understood that she had not gotten that close by accident. Missy had just opened it and was on top of Mila at a full sprint. Her arms were open as she tackled her and used her momentum to carry both of them through the portal.

Mila landed hard on concrete, the impact knocking her weapons out of her hands and the breath from her lungs as Missy slammed onto her and then rolled off.

The void portal blinked out as Mila rolled over and jumped to her feet, already charging, but her arms were suddenly jerked back, and she was lifted into the air. She looked up and saw black tentacles wrapped around her wrists, and as the realization of where she was hit, two more tentacles gripped her ankles. She was easily hoisted up into a spread-eagle position.

Mila looked over as Missy stood up slowly, an evil grin on her face.

"You have done well, pet," the rumbling creaking voice of Azoth said behind Mila's back. "I would have preferred the stronger one, but this one is a prize indeed. Such fun we will have, you and I." He emphasized the last by shaking her violently.

CHAPTER THIRTY-TWO

Cold steel shackles clanked around Mila's wrists. She sucked in a shocked breath as her greatly increased magical potential was cut off like a switch had been flipped.

Her senses were so dull compared to the moment before that she didn't even realize she had been dropped until she hit the floor and crumpled into a heap. She took a few deep breaths to get used to how heavy her body felt without any kind of magic imbuing it. How had she become so used to magic in such a short time? How was this normal for her before she met Finn?

As she looked around, Mila realized she was back in the old factory. The hole she had put into the wall had been reformed, obviously with magic. Mila was surprised to see that Sarah, the Lone Valkyrie Azoth had returned with, was still alive, though unconscious as she hung from the same chains Victoria had earlier.

Missy dropped to her knees and looked up with adoration in her black eyes. "You were so right. Once I used the infernal gift you gave me so long ago, I finally understood."

"I knew you would, pet," Azoth rumbled from behind Mila.

"I need more. I can be your proper weapon. I have no need for this old life. I want the power. I'll do anything for it," Missy begged in a sharp turn from her attitude on the rooftop.

"I am in need of a proper servant." The naked, burnt body of Yaminah hit the floor in front of Mila. "This one was a disappointment."

Mila pushed up to a sitting position to put some distance between herself and the body, its cracked and bleeding skin charred black. Mila had a sudden pang of guilt for doing that to her, but she would have done worse to Mila, given a chance.

Then the body groaned and tried to move.

Mila's eyes went wide. How the hell had she survived an unprotected lightning strike like that? She must have dove through the closest open portal.

"I will not fail you, lord. Please, just give me a bit more power."

The sound of a thousand slithering snakes made Mila's skin crawl. As Azoth came out from behind her, her eyes widened further as she saw him in without a robe for the first time.

His head, arms, and torso were those of a muscular human, though his skin was stone-gray. After that he was all abomination. Instead of legs, he had a mass of black tentacles that had to number in the hundreds. But the most disturbing thing about him was that where a face should be, there was only a never-ending black void. His hood hadn't been dark; this was his actual face. Mila tried to understand how that could even be possible, but quickly found she didn't want to contemplate it.

The Drude slithered up to Missy and held his hand over her face. "My pet does deserve a reward. You shall have it."

A thin black cloud fell from his hand and onto Missy's smiling face. The cloud began to speed up, and it was soon a twisting cyclone as infernal magic was pushed into her.

"Do you know that we Valkyries and you Drude come from a similar origin? Perhaps even the same one." Missy soaked up the magic.

"I did know that."

"There's an interesting theory I once heard from a witch way back when my sisters and I defeated you."

Azoth obviously didn't like the reference to his defeat and began to pull his hand away, but he seemed to be having trouble.

"This witch, he said that if we were in fact from the same source, we were essentially the same beings just created for different purposes."

Azoth was beginning to struggle, trying in vain to pull away. "What are you doing? Stop. I order you to stop!"

Missy slowly stood, the Drude's hand following her. "That got me thinking. What if a Drude and a Valkyrie switched off little bits of their souls? Would you end up with one or the other and have the abilities of both, or something completely different?"

Now Azoth had slithered towards the ground, the strength of his tentacles failing him. His arm stretched out to keep feeding his power to Missy. "No, stop. You can't do this to me. We had a deal!"

"You were never going to fulfill that deal. I knew that from the start, but I needed you to feed me until I could feed myself. And now I can, so I don't need you. I'll consume the rest of your soul, and I will be able to take *myself* off this fucking broken-down piece of garbage. I can go home. I can be free."

Azoth started laughing, which made Missy look down at him sharply. "What is so funny? I'm about to eat your soul."

"You want to leave so badly, but you never asked the question. Why have I not left to return with more of my kind? It's because I can't, Valkyrie. And the best part is that it is all your fault."

"What are you talking about?"

Mila looked over and saw Gram lying not three feet away. If she could just get these cuffs off...

Mila was small, very small, and that came with small wrists. The shackles were a one-size-fits all-design, and for a standard Valkyrie, they would fit. Valkyries were generally tall and well-built women. The smallest one Mila had seen was Missy, and she was still five eight-ish.

Mila tried to pull her hand out. It wouldn't go, but it was close—if she didn't have that thumb in the way.

Azoth laughed again, even with his power being sucked out of him at an alarming rate. "I was defeated by you. Drude do not get defeated, and if we do, our ability to travel the universe is stripped from us. We are cursed to forever live in the place of our shame. I can't travel the stars any more than you can. My death at your hands shut that part of my soul down."

Missy snorted. "Haven't you heard? We Valkyries can fix things like that. Let me just get you into a more agreeable state, shall I?"

She slammed her hands to the sides of his head, then pulled them away. Two more spinning clouds of infernal magic were sucked out of him and formed under her hands.

Azoth screamed in earnest. His head lolled back as his chest heaved and jerked. After two minutes of wailing and crying, the once-fearsome creature finally fell silent. He sagged, although his tentacles kept him from falling over.

Mila pulled as hard as she could, but she just couldn't get the shackle over her thumb. She sighed; she knew what she had to do. With the two of them distracted, it was the perfect time.

Sitting up on her knees, she lifted one knee and awkwardly placed her hand flat on the ground, then tucked her thumb up on top so that when she lowered her knee, it would put all its pressure on the thumb joint. She repeated the process with the other hand.

This was going to suck serious donkey dick, so she didn't want to have to do it twice. This way, she just had to keep from screaming once. Feel that cartilage pop… She didn't want to think about it and rocked forward quickly so all her body weight was on those two joints, which hurt like a son of a bitch but wasn't quite enough pressure.

So she bounced.

That worked, and there was muffled wet pop. Mila screwed her eyes shut as tears ran freely from them. Blood wet her lips after she bit her tongue to keep from screaming.

Very carefully, Mila pulled her hands out. She wanted to be sick, looking at that odd angle on both hands. She had to bite her tongue again when she pulled her hands out one at a time and gently placed the shackles on the concrete so they didn't clink.

As soon as she was clear of the shackles, her magic came rushing back, although noticeably diminished. Immediately she fed power to her hands and nearly cried out as the digits reset themselves. The pain eventually faded as she kept feeding magic to the affected areas. Her tongue was the last thing she healed.

When she looked up, the color drained from Mila's face.

Missy stood over the Drude, her right hand out and open as a rather ordinary hand scythe appeared in it. She gripped it tight and cocked back her arm.

"Let's get that little problem fixed so I can use it myself, shall we?" Missy said to the unconscious Drude.

Her arm swung down but stopped suddenly. She pulled, but it was locked in place. Mila leaned to the side to get a better view.

One of the Drude's tentacles had snaked up to grip the wrist of the hand holding the Reaper.

A crackling laugh filled the echoing factory.

"No. *No!* I took your power." Missy screamed as Azoth slithered to his full height and looked down into her face.

"You really think I didn't know you stole a piece of my soul before you woke me? You think me so incapable?" He ripped the Reaper from her hand and held it up in victory.

"My mission is finally complete! With this, we will become gods. Whatever power we want, we'll just create it. This is the ultimate power in the universe, and you were dumb enough to bring it out around me?"

He laughed again.

Then the wall exploded for the second time that day.

Mila had no clue what was happening, but this was her chance.

As she empowered her body for all it was worth, she snatched up Gram, took one step, and swung hard. The golden sword sliced through Azoth's forearm like it was made of butter and sent the Reaper and attached arm spinning off to land with an odd combination of a wet splat and clanking metal.

Victoria and three other Valkyries Mila had never seen before rushed in, followed closely by Carl and the rest of the team. Azoth looked at his incoming enemies, then at Mila. He reached down with his one remaining hand, palmed Missy's face, and picked her up as a void portal opened.

"I'll be back for that, pet." He turned to the portal, and after a second's consideration, he kicked Yaminah's broken but still living body through the portal, then stepped through himself.

Mila scrambled over to pry Azoth's tentacle hand open, then picked up the Reaper as she muttered to herself.

"This shit just got complicated."

CHAPTER THIRTY-THREE

Finn stepped out of the illusion Freya had kept them in despite him telling her that he knew it was an illusion.

He'd put his hat back on, and his backpack once again held half a ton of treasure. His phone dinged, and he saw there was a message from an unknown number. He hit play and put the phone to his ear to give Freya the entire gambit of emotions in about thirty seconds.

He hung up and turned to her. "Can you teleport?"

"Yes. Why?" she asked suspiciously.

"I need a teleport to San Francisco right now."

Mila and the rest of the team had returned to Victoria's condo, most of them congregating on the roof to perform the cleanup. That involved a lot of magically dissolving bodies. Mila found it telling that not only were the Valkyries efficient at it but so was the G.A.E.L. team.

Mila spoke with Victoria about where to put the Reaper. They couldn't keep it in Elsewhere because Missy could just come in and take it. Victoria didn't want any of the Valkyries to have it because Missy knew where all their homes and hideouts were. Until she could get a new location up and running, the Reaper needed to be somewhere with excellent wards, looked after by capable people.

After two minutes of Victoria dropping not-so-subtle hints, Mila threw up her arms. "Fine! We can keep it at my place. Are you happy?"

Victoria smiled. "Very. Thank you."

A large bubble formed on the deck, to be quickly surrounded by Valkyries. When the teleport bubble popped, no one expected what they got.

Finn, a large floppy yellow sun hat on his head, black Speedo barely visible, and flip-flops on his feet, shouted a war cry, Fragar held above his head. The small darkly tanned woman who had brought him jumped backward with a squeak and immediately teleported away.

Finn, on realizing there were no enemies to fight, deflated, spotted Mila, and jogged over. He collapsed Fragar and, for some ungodly reason, stuffed it down the front of his very tight and already full Speedo.

"Oh, my God, Finn!" Mila's mouth kept working, but no more words came out.

He struck a pose. "You like em? It's like I'm wearing nothing!"

"Yup, sure is, babe. Nothing at all," Mila agreed.

Remmy walked by and turned just as she passed his crotch.

"I can totally see your balls, dude," she remarked.

With a toothy grin, she bounced over to help Howard pack up the weapons.

Finn looked down at his package. "It's not *that* bad."

"Well, I can't say I don't like it in theory." Mila chuckled.

Another teleport bubble appeared, to be surrounded once again, but when it popped, it revealed Penny and a very tired woman with a blue pixie cut. The woman waved to Mila and held her hand up like a telephone. Mila waved back and gave a thumbs-up while Penny flew over.

Rebecca teleported away, and Penny dropped a very heavy softball-sized device into Mila's hand.

"Is this it?"

Penny nodded as her eyes drooped in exhaustion. She flew over to Finn and laid on his shoulder to fall asleep.

Finn looked at her on his shoulder. "What, no hello?"

"Sheeir skee," she mumbled.

"You can *not* see my balls in these trunks!" Finn scowled.

Remmy walked past in the opposite direction. "At this point, those trunks *are* your balls."

"I fucking hate you guys."

Mila gave him a pouty face as she walked over and slipped her arms around him. "Poor babe. It's okay, I love you."

"Love you too, darlin'. So, you like the trunks?"

"Oh, no, babe. Those things are awful. You can totally see your balls."

The End
(for now)

Mila has a lot to process: her new powers, betrayal, Finn's swimwear choices... But the one that takes the cake is what to do with the Reaper. It's not every day you're responsible for one of the most powerful artifacts in the universe.

How do you hide something that important? Sometimes the best hiding places just don't exist.

Join Mila and Finn as they discover what it takes to keep a planet safe in *Wings of the Valkyrie*, book three of the Lone Valkyrie series.

P.S. I hope you like baby dragons...

Get sneak peeks, exclusive giveaways, behind the scenes content, and more.
PLUS you'll be notified of special **one day only fan pricing** on new releases.

Sign up today to get free stories.

CLICK HERE

or visit: https://marthacarr.com/read-free-stories/

AUTHOR NOTES - CHARLEY CASE
APRIL 4, 2020

This book was interesting to write. I started it when the country was doing great; strong economy, the seasons were changing from winter to spring, and the new beers were coming out at my favorite brewery. By the time I wrote The End the government had closed the country down and we were getting the first hints of what life would be like closeted in our homes for the foreseeable future.

I have to be honest here... if I wasn't married to a woman who payed attention to the world at large, I might not have noticed there was a pandemic going on.

Life as an author is a strange and wonderful thing, at least if you're an introvert with an overactive imagination. But with that life comes a lot of isolation.

A week into the social distancing someone asked me how I was coping with all the changes. What I said was, "It's been a little hard, but if we stick to the plan we'll get back on track before you know it." What I wanted to say was, "Coping with what?" But, I can't really say that; not if I don't want to sound like an asshole.

I live in a world that starts at 7:30 am when I wake up and make a cup of tea, then I write until 4:30 pm when I stop to make dinner. Me and the wife take a walk, maybe workout, then watch a TV show or a movie. I'm in bed around 11:00 pm and the whole thing starts over. I can do that for weeks... I prefer to do that for weeks. I'm actually built for social isolation.

But I'm not so far gone that I don't realize that you are, more than likely, not.

So, I would like to take this opportunity to share with you a few tips to get you through this trying time. After all, if you want to know how to fix your car you would ask a mechanic, right? Well, if you want to know how to survive isolation, ask a writer.

Tip 1: Never think of yourself as being trapped; you're not. You are the opposite of trapped, you're finally free. You no longer have to worry about what people are going to think of you when you leave the house; no need to get dressed up, put on makeup, or wear that fake smile you have to use at the office. You get to be you, in all your weird and quirky ways, and no one will be able to judge you... except you. Which leads to my second tip.

Tip 2: This isolation will be the only time some of you will have to really take a close look at yourself in the raw, as it were. This was the hardest part for me. After that first month of gloriously wearing pajama pants everyday, and eating whatever I liked for lunch regardless of bad my breath might be afterward, I had a nice long sit down with myself and evaluated my life choices.

I was an animal... a big stinky animal. My wife is a saint.

Tip 3: Don't judge yourself too harshly, we all need a break and if that break makes us look like an ape that broke into the banana bin and gorged ourselves into a banana fueled coma, that's okay. Life is a big ass ball of stress, and we need to decompress. But there is a big difference between not judging ourselves too harshly, and not judging ourselves at all.

We are our own keepers. That means we are the masters of our own destinies, but it means we're the masters of our own faults as well. Notice those faults, don't dwell on them, just mark them down and think about them. We are born the way we are right now, we learned all the things we do over a lifetime; it's going to take a minute to reorganize.

Tip 4: Make a list. After that first month I realized there were a few things I didn't like about how I was carrying on. It wasn't fair to me or my body or my wife. I needed to make a few changes. So, I made a list of the things I would like to see improve in my life, and when I was done that list was waaaaaaayyyy too long.

So I picked the top three things, and threw the rest in a drawer. Once I had my much smaller list I moved to the next stage.

Tip 5: Make a plan. I drew up elaborate plans to change those three things over night. I was going to be a fucking golden god! No one has ever seen change like this, this fast, and this effective. I was going to blow my own socks off, then wash them and fold them and put them in the sock drawer, then blow the sock drawer out of the dresser.

That lasted about twenty minutes.

Once reality hit, I realized that any step in the right

direction was one step I hadn't taken yesterday. So I rewrote my plan to the most pathetic version of itself. For example, I need to exercise. Well, I wasn't going to do that, so instead I put "walk to the mailbox everyday when the mail truck comes."

And I did. Then I did it the next day, and the next. The whole time I was thinking that it was exercise, and that made me feel foolish, so I decided that I could handle a walk around the block, and started doing that.

See what I mean, pathetically small plan, but it was miles more than I was doing.

Tip 6: Go outside. You need the sunlight to make Vitamin D. We all need the D, go do it. You'll feel better, promise.

Tip 7: It's over before you know it.

Why did I just tell you to go make yourself better? Because that's how you go for a long time in isolation. You get a project, you work on the project, and before you know it a few months have gone by and you hardly notice.

The secondary benefit is that you actually got shit done! You're going to be home anyway, may as well make the most out of it.

Tip 8: Have fun. Call your friends and talk on the phone, or over video chat. This is the perfect time to reconnect with the friends that you don't call all that often because you know they're home too. Play cards, play music, play hide and go seek with the dog.

Tip 9: I don't know what the hell I'm talking about. Seriously, I'm a guy who makes shit up all day, what the hell do I know? My whole point is that this is not a time to spiral down, it's a time to spiral up.

Make that happen however you make that happen. Just make it happen.

Well, the sun is going down, and I have a cat on a leash that wants to take a walk…

I hope you all are doing well and doing your part. I know it's been hard, but with a plan you'll get through this before you know it.

P.S. Wash your hands. Right now, go do it.

Charley Case
(*My house,*
Boise, Idaho
4/4/2020)

Week bajillion of the quarantine (probably fifth week in reality) and successes so far – figured out how to use my sewing machine after a few decades and fits and starts, walking 3.15 miles – basically a 5k, have joined a zoom yoga class, went to some neighborhood zoom happy hours with games and have made a baker's dozen bandanas for some nurses. Somewhere in there finished writing a book and read two third's of Splendid and the Vile by Erik Larson about Churchill before the U.S. joined the war. It's soothing because in this one I know who wins and when it all ends.

Not bad overall.

This week I hope to add in meditation, stay away from the news, (both of those are for the sake of sanity), and sketch some drawings for the mural I'm doing down the hallway. That's right, I'm drawing a large, complicated mural down my long hallway. Rather than adopt the pristine look of an HGTV makeover, I'm going for making the house look singularly like my own. I'll share pics and videos when it's underway and as the process continues.

I used to draw cartoons of families and their pets as a side gig a long time ago and drew cartoons of Louie, the Offspring, when he was little to assume him. This is just a return to some roots.

I'm also doing a fairly big embroidery of flowers that I have plans to frame for the dining room. I can't buy plants right now or start that vegetable garden, so I think it's coming out sideways in the artwork. That works for the time being. Maybe I'll end up with the feeling of a continuous garden from the indoors to the outside. I could live with that.

My future daughter in law, Jackie Venson and the Offspring have been doing nightly Facebook Live concerts at 9 pm CT, which is a lot of expended energy, but has also provided an audience in the thousands, and growing, something fun to do seven days a week. Amazing.

One thing I've had reinforced for me as an entire world is in time out, is that we're very clever people who will go to great lengths to find ways to connect, to be creative, to structure our days and to find meaning in what's happening – good or bad. That's why I know we'll make it through this too. And with a lot of stories to tell our grandchildren. More adventures to follow.

If smart phones and GPS rule the world - why am I hunting a magic compass to save the planet?

Austin Detective Maggie Parker has seen some weird things in her day, but finding a surly gnome rooting through her garage beats all.

Her world is about to be turned upside down in a frantic search for 4 Elementals.

Each one has an artifact that can keep the Earth humming along, but they need her to unite them first.

Unless the forces against her get there first.

OTHER BOOKS IN THE TERRANAVIS UNIVERSE

The Adventures of Maggie Parker Series

The Witches of Pressler Street

The Adventures of Finnegan Dragonbender

Other books by Martha Carr

Other books by Charley Case

JOIN THE TERRANAVIS UNIVERSE FACEBOOK GROUP

FOLLOW TERRANAVIS UNIVERSE ON FACEBOOK

CONNECT WITH THE AUTHORS

Martha Carr Social

Website:
http://www.marthacarr.com

Facebook:
https://www.facebook.com/groups/MarthaCarrFans/

https://www.facebook.com/terranavisuniverse/

Michael Anderle Social

Michael Anderle Social
Website:
http://www.lmbpn.com

Email List:
http://lmbpn.com/email/

Facebook
https://www.facebook.com/TheKurtherianGambitBooks/